MEET THE GIRL TALK CHARACTERS

Sabrina Wells is petite, with curly auburn hair, sparkling hazel eyes, and a bubbly personality. Sabrina loves magazines, shopping, sleepovers, and most of all, she loves talking to her best friends.

Katie Campbell is a straight-A student and super athlete. With her blond hair, blue eyes, and matching clothes, she's everyone's idea of little miss perfect. But Katie has a few surprises for everyone, including herself!

Randy Zak has just moved to Acorn Falls from New York City, and is she ever cool! With her radical spiked haircut and her hip New York clothes, Randy teaches everyone just how much fun it is to be different.

Allison Cloud is a Native American Indian. Allison's super smart and really beautiful. But she has one major problem: She's thirteen years old, five foot seven, and still growing!

Here's what they're talking about in
Girl Talk

KATIE: Hello. Katie speaking.

SABRINA: Katie! It's me, Sabs! And you're not going to believe what I just found out!

KATIE: What?

SABRINA: Guess who's going to be staying at Oak Park Hotel while we're there. Just guess!

KATIE: Who? Is it someone we know?

SABRINA: It's definitely someone we want to meet! And he's only going to be in Minneapolis for one weekend!

KATIE: Sabs! You don't mean . . . Dylan Palmer is staying at the same hotel we are?

SABRINA: Yes! Yes! Can you believe it!

ROCKIN' CLASS TRIP

By L. E. Blair

GIRL TALK® series created by Western Publishing Company, Inc.

Western Publishing Company, Inc., Racine, Wisconsin 53404

Text by Carol McCarren

Chapter One

It was almost the end of English class and Ms. Staats was writing our homework assignment on the blackboard. It was the usual Wednesday assignment. We had to study our word power list for the vocabulary quiz we always had on Thursday.

"Word power is the worst," I whispered to one of my best friends, Katie Campbell.

"Maybe we can study together after school, Sabs," Katie whispered back.

I was about to say, "Good idea," when a crackly, static sound came over the public address system.

"Please quiet down," Ms. Staats said. "There's an announcement."

Then the voice we all know so well at Bradley Junior High said, "Your attention, please. This is your principal, Mr. Hansen. There will be a special assembly tomorrow during third period for all seventh graders. Report to your homerooms, as usual. Your teacher will escort your class to the auditorium. That's tomorrow, third period. Thank you."

That was all. But it was plenty, I thought. Our entire grade was in trouble, and it wasn't hard to figure out why.

The bell rang, signaling the end of the period, and Ms. Staats said we could go. Out in the hallway it was the usual wild scene between classes, with books, papers, and even a few people flying in all directions.

Katie and I walked over to the locker we shared. I took out my lunch and switched my morning books for the ones I needed in the afternoon. Katie did the same and then I slammed the door closed.

"Hey, Sabs! Watch out!" Katie said, looking absolutely horrified.

"What's the matter?" I looked down to see what she was pointing at. It was a photograph of Dylan Palmer. Or actually half a photograph, sticking out of our locker door. Now, that was *truly* an emergency for me.

Dylan Palmer is my absolute favorite rock star of all time. I have pictures of him everywhere —

in my room, pasted inside my notebook covers, and, naturally, inside my locker. And I know everything about him from reading *Hip Teen* magazine and *Rock Beat*.

Poor Dylan looked so pathetic with his gorgeous face folded in half that I just dropped my books right on the floor and yanked the door open to get him out.

"Oh, no," I sighed as I tried to smooth out the creases. "He's really smashed."

"Gee — too bad," Katie said sympathetically. "Maybe it will flatten out if you stick it in your math book."

"Hey — good idea!" I slipped the photo inside the thick textbook and we started walking to the cafeteria. "I guess Mr. Hansen's announcement really got me rattled."

"Me too," Katie agreed. "Did you notice the way he said *special* assembly?"

"Yeah — assembly of doom is what he really meant," I said.

You see, we were all really worried that Mr. Hansen was going to call off the class trip to Minneapolis. Our whole grade had been talking about this trip for weeks and we were all set to go next weekend. But now . . . well, I for one was pretty sure that we had blown it. The seventh-grade class was definitely in trouble.

It had all started on Monday, when Mr. Hansen announced that special visitors were coming in to observe the seventh grade during the week. I didn't know exactly what that was supposed to mean. But just hearing the word *observe* made me feel like one of those frogs we had to dissect in biology lab.

Anyway, Mr. Hansen asked us to be on our best behavior while the visitors were here. But I guess there were some characters in our class who thought this would be the perfect time to start acting up.

They got to work pretty quickly, too. When I got to school Tuesday morning, the first thing I noticed was that somebody had climbed up to the roof of the school and stolen the letters that spelled out BRADLEY JUNIOR HIGH SCHOOL. They didn't take all the letters, though. Just the B and the LEY from BRADLEY. So now the front of our school reads: RAD JUNIOR HIGH SCHOOL. And nobody knows who did it.

Mr. Hansen was standing on the front steps of the school, staring up at the letters. I could tell he was really angry.

Then, on Wednesday, the entire seventh grade had to watch some dumb movie for our health class. I think the movie was from the 1960s or something. It was all about relationships, and growing up, and being responsible, and junk like that.

It was really supercorny and sort of fake. I mean, no matter what happened, all the kids in it kept smiling these big, fake smiles. They looked like robot kids or something. Like, there was one part where this boy broke up with his girlfriend. You just knew she was really upset and could have burst into tears, but she just kept smiling through the whole thing. It was so stupid that the whole class just cracked up.

Ms. Nelson, our health teacher, stopped the film to ask us why we were laughing. But nobody said anything. Ms. Nelson got this stern expression on her face and said that she had expected more mature behavior from seventh graders.

After that I tried to take the film seriously, but it didn't help. There's nothing worse than trying to look serious when you're really laughing hysterically inside. So the whole seventh grade ended up sitting there holding our stomachs and doing this silent laugh, with our faces turning all red — like we were about to explode. It was really crazy.

To make things even worse, a couple of boys started throwing spitballs at the screen. I'm almost sure it was my twin brother, Sam, who started it. He's always doing dumb stuff like that.

That was it. The whole auditorium started cracking up again . . . out loud! And when the spitballs starting sticking to the screen, we were totally out of control! You'd see a close-up of this dorky smiling kid, and there would be all these spitballs hanging off his face. It really looked gross, but all we could do was laugh.

When the lights came on at the end of the film, Ms. Nelson stood up and looked at us.

"Ladies and gentlemen," she said softly, "I'm very disappointed in you."

She didn't say anything else, but she didn't have to. Ms. Nelson is one of the coolest teachers at Bradley. She's young, and black, and she used to be a model in New York. She's more like a friend than a teacher, really. I felt really bad about the way I had acted. And so did the rest of the class. But it was too late to do anything about it.

Considering everything that had happened

this week, it didn't take a rocket scientist to figure out what tomorrow's assembly would be about. Katie seemed pretty worried about it, too.

"Mr. Hansen must be really mad," Katie said. "I wonder what he'll do to us tomorrow."

"Don't sweat it, Katie," a familiar voice said from right behind me. When I turned my head, I saw another of my best friends, Randy Zak, right behind us in the hall.

"And why would they blame the whole seventh grade?" Randy added as we walked into the cafeteria. "It just doesn't make sense."

Randy's from New York City, and she's really cool. She always helps me calm down when I get upset about something. She sort of helps me see the other side of things. My mom calls it "putting things into perspective."

"Right," I replied as we sat down at our usual table. "How do they know it wasn't an eighth grader or a ninth grader who stole those letters?"

"Probably because the word *rad* is part of our class slogan," Allison Cloud, my other best friend, piped in as she joined us.

We all looked at Al and then started to chant:

> *"The seventh grade*
> *can never fade*
> *we're totally rad*
> *we're superbad*
> *at Braaad —*
> *ley Junior High!"*

We all collapsed in giggles, and it took a few seconds for us to stop laughing.

"You know, you're right, Al," I said when I managed to catch my breath. "The eighth and ninth graders don't use the word *rad* half as much as we do."

Then Katie said something that absolutely shocked us: "I hope Mr. Hansen doesn't cancel the class trip." She slowly took her lunch out of her book bag. I couldn't help noticing that it was a sandwich wrapped in foil and a banana.

For a minute no one said anything. I guess we were all worried that Katie might be right.

Wait a minute, I thought to myself, you're acting like the trip is already canceled! I looked at my best friends. All three of them were looking pretty down. I decided to try to cheer them up.

"Hey, listen. I've got an idea. If we don't get to go on the trip next weekend, we can do something else. We could have a sleepover on Saturday. And Sunday we could all go —"

I was *about* to say roller blading at the new Acorn Blades roller rink when an all-too-familiar voice spoke up behind me.

"All go where?" the voice asked.

"This is a private conversation," I announced without even turning around. I just knew that stuck-up Stacy Hansen was standing right behind me. She's the principal's daughter and she's a *total* phony.

"Sorry," Stacy said sweetly. "I thought I knew what you girls were talking about."

"Well, you don't," Randy replied, spinning around to face Stacy.

"Hey, cute outfit, Stacy," Randy said sarcastically. "Looks like you just jogged into a giant wad of bubble gum!" Which made us crack up laughing because it happened to be true.

Stacy was wearing a hot-pink jogging outfit with a fancy designer emblem on the jacket pocket. And, of course, she was wearing a pair of designer pink tennis shoes that must have cost about ninety dollars. Obviously she was going to Acorn Sports, the posh health club, after school. And obviously she wanted everyone to know it.

"Don't worry, girls," Stacy's best friend, Eva Malone, chimed in. "We didn't come over here to talk to you. We just came to get Stacy's concert tickets," Eva continued.

"Yeah, they flew off her tray and landed right under Sabrina's seat," another of Stacy's friends, B.Z. Latimer exclaimed as she bent down to look under my chair.

Eva, B.Z., and another girl, Laurel Spencer, are all part of Stacy's stuck-up clique. Needless to say, our group and Stacy's group are not the best of friends.

But I hadn't seen any tickets "fly" by. Obviously Stacy Hansen was setting us up for a major news flash. I just knew I was going to hate it.

"We wouldn't want to lose these babies," Eva said. "Everybody knows the Dylan Palmer concert is totally sold out."

"Dylan Palmer!" I yelped. I bolted out of my chair, knocking it back into Stacy.

For a minute there, it seemed like the whole cafeteria was looking in our direction.

"You got tickets to the Dylan Palmer concert in Minneapolis! That's impossible!" I exclaimed breathlessly.

Even as the words were coming out of my mouth, I was sorry I was saying them. It was just the reaction Stacy had been looking for.

Of course, anyone who knows anything about me knows that I would give just about anything to see him in person. ANYTHING! I'm the biggest Dylan Palmer fan in the entire universe! And creepy Stacy Hansen and company were going to see him in concert instead of me! It just wasn't fair.

"Are you sure you've got all five?" B.Z. asked loudly, peering over Stacy's shoulder.

Stacy deliberately fanned the tickets out in front of her face.

By this time a crowd of kids had gathered around us. Me and my big mouth. This was just the audience Stacy had been looking for. But I still couldn't believe she had those tickets. Dylan Palmer's one and only appearance in Minneapolis had sold out in less than two hours after the tickets went on sale. And that had been more than a month ago!

"One . . . two . . . three . . . four . . . *five*," Stacy counted out loud. "Front row, center," she added in a sugary-sweet voice.

"Front row, center," I mumbled under my

breath, along with about twenty other kids. I thought I was going to die right on the spot.

"You know, Eva," Stacy continued, as if there was no one else around, "I've got five tickets here . . . and there are only four of us."

Suddenly the whole crowd seemed to come to attention, breathlessly waiting for Stacy's next words. What was she going to do with that extra ticket? Maybe, just maybe . . .

"Nice acting job, Stacy," Randy cut in suddenly. "But just for the record, did you guys rehearse this? Or do you just improvise as you go along?"

Stacy's face turned bright red as everyone burst out laughing. I sighed in relief. Leave it to Randy to break Stacy's spell over the crowd.

"Don't you think they deserve a hand?" Randy asked the crowd, clapping her hands.

We all applauded and Stacy's mood did a total turnaround. She looked just like Mr. Hansen had when he was standing in front of the school on Monday, staring at the place where the stolen letters had been. Her big brown eyes became narrow slits, and you could practically see the smoke coming out of her ears.

"You're going to wish you had never said

that, Randy Zak!" she fumed. "You think you're so cool, with that . . . that porcupine haircut!"

Everyone I knew thought Randy's spiked haircut was really cool, so I didn't think that Stacy had scored any points with that line.

"At least it's a style from this *century*!" Randy retorted, making everyone laugh. "You think you're such a big shot with your front-row tickets? Well, here's some news for you, Stacy Hansen . . . nobody cares."

As soon as I heard Randy say "nobody cares," I felt a big knot in my stomach and stared down at the floor.

"I know *one* person who cares," Stacy said slowly. And I knew she was staring right at me.

Chapter Two

When I looked up from the floor, everyone was staring at me — especially Stacy.

I knew if I didn't say something fast, she would. I wanted to sound really cool and like I didn't care one tiny bit about the Dylan Palmer tickets. But I couldn't seem to find my brain — or my voice.

Finally I just looked straight at Stacy's smirking face. It was probably only for a couple of seconds. But it felt like a hundred years.

"What makes you think I care about your stupid tickets, Stacy?" I blurted out.

"C'mon, Sabrina. You expect me to believe you wouldn't give just about anything to get your hot little hands on just *one* of these tickets?" Stacy jeered as she fanned the tickets in front of my nose.

That did it. I don't know what came over me, but all of a sudden I just reached across the table

14

and grabbed Katie's banana. Before I could stop myself, I looked up at Stacy and said, "Stacy Hansen, all I'd give you for those tickets is . . . is . . . this *banana*!"

When I realized what I had said, I felt like a total jerk. I just stood there, holding out that stupid banana.

But, surprisingly, everyone else seemed to think I had given Stacy exactly the answer she deserved.

"Way to go, Sabrina!" someone in the crowd yelled out.

"Throw it at her!" another voice yelled above the laughter.

"*Excellent!*" someone else chimed in.

The whole crowd started chanting, "THROW IT! THROW IT! THROW IT!"

But I couldn't do it. Out of nowhere, I saw a piece of chocolate cream pie flying through the air and heading straight for us. I ducked. But I heard Stacy scream. It hit her right on top of the head. Everyone started laughing, and the next thing I knew, there was food flying everywhere.

People were throwing mashed potatoes, peas, sandwiches, forkfuls of beef stew, fruit salad, potato chips — anything they could get their hands on. My twin brother, Sam, and his friends Nick Robbins, Greg Loggins, and Jason McKee climbed up on top of their table and started yelling, "FOOD FIGHT! FOOD FIGHT!"

The whole cafeteria was in a total frenzy — laughing, throwing food, and having a great time.

Even Katie and Allison were cracking up and throwing bits of food at each other. The class nerd, Winslow Barton, was shaking up cans of soda and spraying everyone in sight. The cafeteria workers were ducking behind the cash registers and the food counter for cover.

All of the adults in the cafeteria were yelling at us, but we didn't listen. But everyone noticed when Mr. Hansen walked through the door with a lady and two men in business suits wearing blue HELLO, MY NAME IS stickers.

We all froze and just stared at them. It was like one of those stop-action frames you see on TV during sports shows. I knew right away that the people with Mr. Hansen were the special visitors he had told us about.

They all had the strangest expressions on their faces and just stood there, gazing around, like they had just landed on another planet.

Mr. Hansen glared at us, turned on his heel, and left. Then the visitors followed. That gave me the creeps. If Mr. Hansen was too mad to yell at us, he was definitely too mad to let us go to Minneapolis next weekend.

But it was even creepier when none of our teachers said a word about the food fight, either. The whole afternoon went by, and all our teachers kept acting like nothing had happened. But every time we left a classroom, we heard the same thing:

"Don't forget. Special assembly tomorrow."

I kept wishing that someone would just yell at us or something. Even that would have been better than not saying anything at all. I was absolutely positive that Mr. Hansen was going to cancel the class trip. So why couldn't he just tell us and get it over with? The suspense was driving me crazy! It was driving the whole seventh grade crazy!

Finally the afternoon came to an end. Randy, Al, Katie, and I decided that we would all go straight home.

All I could think about was the special assembly. I even dreamed about it that night. In the dream all the seventh-grade teachers were standing on the stage in the auditorium. They were throwing broccoli and spitballs at the seventh graders, who were sitting in the seats. Mr. Hansen was standing at the podium. He kept saying, "Rad Junior High School, ha ha ha," over and over again. It was the most bizarre dream I had ever had.

It was pretty hard to get through Thursday morning at school. First and second period seemed to take forever.

When third period came, Ms. Staats took attendance, then led our homeroom into the auditorium.

All our teachers looked pretty solemn, even Mr. Grey. He's my social studies teacher and he's really gorgeous. He looks like a soap opera star or something, and he always has a smile for everyone. But today he just had this blank expression on his face.

"Gee, these teachers could lighten up a little. It looks like the Supreme Court in here," Randy whispered to me as we walked down the aisle.

"We must really be in big trouble," I replied without moving my lips.

"I didn't know you knew ventriloquism," Randy commented without moving her lips.

I almost started to laugh, but Miss Munson's shrill voice quickly brought me back to reality. Miss Munson's my math teacher. She's one of the oldest, grouchiest teachers at Bradley and she loves to give pop quizzes. Needless to say, she isn't one of my favorites.

"Come along, ladies! Be seated," she snapped, ushering the four of us into the nearest row. "Mr. Hansen's about to begin."

I looked at Katie and Allison. Katie raised her eyebrows as if to say, "I told you so." Allison had her head down and seemed to be inspecting her fingernails. I could tell everyone was really nervous.

I turned around and spotted Sam's red head a couple of rows behind us. He was sitting with his friends Greg Loggins and Jason McKee. Even they looked kind of worried. And that's a pretty unusual sight.

We all sat in silence and watched Mr. Hansen walk up to the podium in the middle of the stage. It felt like everyone in the auditorium was holding their breath at the same time. Mr. Hansen cleared his throat and it echoed through the whole auditorium.

"I don't think this special assembly comes as

a surprise to any of you," he began.

We all shifted uncomfortably in our seats.

Mr. Hansen puckered his lips, squinted his eyes, and stared out at us. I noticed again how much he and Stacy looked alike when they were mad. He waited until everyone had stopped squirming and the room was quiet again.

"It seems that the majority of you have forgotten that there are rules and regulations to be followed in this school," he went on, putting his hands on the podium and leaning forward.

"I wonder if he's including Stacy in the 'majority,'" I whispered to Katie under my breath.

She rolled her eyes as if to say "no way."

"Would any of you like to tell me where the unruly behavior is coming from?" Mr. Hansen asked, raising his voice.

"I'm waiting!" Mr. Hansen bellowed. He took a step back and crossed his arms in front of his chest.

By this time it was pretty obvious that Mr. Hansen had big plans for us. You could tell he really didn't expect an answer to his question. He just wanted us to think about it for a while.

We all squirmed in our seats and waited. He

seemed to take forever to say his next words.

"We are your teachers . . ." he began.

"Major news flash," Randy whispered.

". . . and up until this point, we have been very proud of our seventh-grade class. So proud, in fact, that we even allowed you to plan a weekend trip to Minneapolis," he went on. "But today I am here to tell you that we no longer feel any pride in our seventh graders."

Mr. Hansen went on and on, telling us how we had no manners, no respect for public property, no sense of responsibility, and basically that we were just a bunch of rowdy, wild kids who were going to grow up to be rowdy, wild adults.

He talked about the food fight, the letters missing from the front of the school, and the way we had behaved at that dumb movie. He used all these big adjectives like "atrocious," "inexcusable," and "totally reprehensible." He was making us sound like major criminals or something.

I was really trying hard to listen, but after a while my thoughts wandered. I started to think about a new Dylan Palmer song, called "Outrageous, Contagious Love," and I started wondering if Dylan Palmer got into much trouble when he was in seventh grade. It was hard to imagine a cool guy like him in a food fight. Then I started thinking about Stacy's dumb tickets and about missing the concert.

I didn't get into a mood about it, though, because Mr. Hansen finally said something about the class trip. I sat up straight in my seat and started listening again.

"As you already know," Mr. Hansen was saying, "part of the funding for your class trip was coming directly from the Board of Education. The board was generous enough to give us a grant so that the seventh grade could visit our fair city of Minneapolis.

"The schedule was going to be presented by representatives of the Board of Education during this special assembly," he went on. "That's why three members of the board came to visit our school this week . . . to see how well behaved you . . . WERE!" Mr. Hansen said emphatically, his face bright red.

"Oh, no!" I moaned softly. No wonder Mr. Hansen was so upset! The three visitors from the Board of Education had walked into the middle of the biggest food fight in the history of Bradley Junior High! I had always been proud that I was president of the seventh grade, but right now I just wanted to sink into the floor.

"Of course, there is no way we can reward you for good behavior," Mr. Hansen boomed. "There is no way we can send you off for a weekend of fun and pleasure. Because you've got to learn that there's more to life than fun and pleasure!"

Then he took a step forward, as if he was going to say something really incredible.

"There's . . . manners!" he shouted at the top of his lungs.

"Oh, brother," Allison muttered. Then she let out a tiny gasp and we all stared at her. I would have started laughing if Mr. Hansen hadn't been talking about the class trip.

"But since the preparations have been made," our principal continued in a quieter tone, "we have decided to proceed with our plans for this trip."

I turned to look at Katie, just as she turned to look at me. Both of us were grinning from ear to ear, and so were Randy and Al. I spun around and looked at Sam, who was giving me the "thumbs up" sign and nodding his head in approval. Everyone started murmuring in excitement. The mood in the auditorium had completely changed.

"However —" Mr. Hansen bellowed.

The murmuring stopped abruptly and the entire seventh grade looked up at our principal. We were hanging on his next word.

"— our planned pleasure excursion will now be a working trip. I hope you will all learn an important lesson about the real world," he added in a grim tone.

Mr. Hansen then went on to explain what he meant.

During our weekend in Minneapolis, we were going to stay at the Oak Park Hotel. It's one of the biggest and most beautiful hotels in the city. We were going to tour the city, visit museums, and see a live theater production of Shakespeare's *Macbeth*.

"Did I just hear what I think I heard?" I asked Randy in a whisper. "A fancy hotel, sightseeing, and a play?"

"If that's the real world, let me at it!" Randy responded with a quick grin.

Did Mr. Hansen really think this was going to punish us? I didn't know about everybody else, but it sounded pretty good to me! Especially the part about the play. I want to be an actress someday, and I've never seen a live play in a big city. I couldn't believe it!

Next Mr. Hansen told us about the daytime activities. The original plan had been to take us to WildWorld, the biggest amusement park in Minnesota. But now we were going to go to the Science Museum and the Minneapolis Institute of Arts instead. Even that didn't sound too bad to me. There were some other things planned, too, but I was so excited about the play, I didn't hear all of them.

The catch to all this was that we were going to be graded on the whole trip. At first that didn't make any sense to me at all. But then it started to sink in. We were going to be tested on the things we learned on each of the "educational" portions of the trip. And we were going to be graded on our manners during the whole weekend.

In preparation for the trip, we would have to take special classes after school during the coming week. The classes would be held every day except for Friday, when we would actually leave. But I didn't let that bother me for a second. The only thing I cared about was that we were still going to Minneapolis!

After Mr. Hansen finished, Miss Miller got up and announced that our first assignment was to bring in a packed suitcase on Monday. Then, after checking with Mr. Hansen, she said that the assembly was over, and we were dismissed.

The whole class was in high gear. Like, you just knew we really just wanted to start bouncing off the walls. But we were all being careful not to get too rowdy.

"Mr. Hansen must be absolutely crazy," Randy said with a laugh when we got out into the hallway.

"It doesn't make any sense, but who cares!" I said, throwing my arms out wide.

"It's just too good to be true," Katie kept saying.

"Well, you know what they say," Allison cut in. "If you think it's too good to be true, it probably is."

We all looked at her like she had two heads or something.

"Well, don't forget about those special classes we have to take next week," she reminded us.

"Like 'How to Pack a Suitcase'?" Randy laughed. "Give me a break. It's a no-brainer."

I was thinking about that part, too. But

besides packing a suitcase, the special classes we had to take the following week were on topics like manners, respect, and responsibility.

"I hope they're all that easy," Katie muttered, changing the mood again. "He did say that our grade for the trip is worth twenty-five percent of our health class grade. That's an awful lot."

"You're not kidding." Allison sighed as the warning bell rang.

"Well, I'm not going to let this stuff ruin my fun," Randy cut in. "It'll be great to spend some time in a big city, even if it's just for a few days."

"Randy's right," I said. "How hard could it be?"

But a little voice inside was telling me that this might not be as easy as Randy thought. I just kept thinking about our teachers' faces during the assembly. They sure looked like we were in for some serious business.

I was glad the weekend was coming soon. I was beginning to think that we'd really need Saturday and Sunday to rest up for next week.

Chapter Three

I figured that packing a suitcase was going to be easy — a real no-brainer, like Randy had said — so I put off doing it for the whole weekend. But on Sunday night, when I finally got started, I found out it was a lot harder than I expected.

The only times I ever had to pack anything were when I went camping or when I went on a sleepover. I had definitely never packed for a weekend trip to the city before. I spent hours deciding what to bring.

There was no way my tote bag was going to be able to hold everything, so I had to borrow a suitcase from my mom. It was huge and bright orange. And it had all these stickers all over it from trips my parents took before we were born. Some even said stuff like PEACE and LOVE. I wasn't too thrilled with it, but I didn't really have a choice.

When I got to school on Monday, I met Katie

at our locker. She had brought a sleek tan suit-case that belonged to her big sister, Emily. It was so compact, Katie was even able to fit it in our locker. Meanwhile I had to carry my orange monster around all day. I felt like I was dragging around a circus trunk.

All of the special classes were being held in the cafeteria after school. After seventh period, our last class, I met my friends in the hall and we walked over to the cafeteria together.

When we got there, the place looked a little strange — just a hint of what was to come. All the tables were arranged in a giant horseshoe, and in the middle there was a portable black-board with writing all over it.

All our teachers stood near the blackboard, looking just as serious as they had in the assem-bly.

The word AGENDA was written out across the top of the blackboard. Below it a list read:

DAY ONE:
ORIENTATION
ORGANIZATION: How to Pack a Suitcase
DAY TWO:
RESPONSIBILITY: Planning and Promptness

RESPONSIBILITY: Following Instructions
DAY THREE:
GROOMING: Proper Attire
SPEECH: Correct Use of Language
DAY FOUR:
RESPECT: Public Property
RESPECT: Proper Attitude

"This looks like it's going to be a *ton* of work," I mumbled under my breath to my friends as we walked in together.

"A little more than just saying please and thank you," Randy agreed.

We were barely inside the cafeteria doorway when Mr. Grey walked over to us.

"Please take your place in line, girls," he said.

Then I noticed that the walls were posted with big letters corresponding to our last names, and everyone was lined up in alphabetical order around the room. And they didn't look too happy about it, either!

That meant that the four of us would be split up. "Campbell" and "Cloud" were on one side, and "Wells" and "Zak" were all the way on the other side. Also, we had to be lined up boy-girl-boy-girl. That put me right in front of my painin-the-neck brother Sam!

"I had a feeling you'd drop in." He smiled as I fell into line, dragging my suitcase behind me.

"Suitcases must be lined up in front of each person," Miss Miller announced. "Identification tags must be in full view at all times," she continued. "Please remove any former travel tags at this time."

"Man, she sounds like a robot," Sam whispered as we bent down to remove the old tags. I hadn't even thought about putting an identification tag on my suitcase. With all those stickers and colors, why would I need one?

Just then I noticed that Sam and I had the exact same orange suitcases, except mine was a lot bigger. I hadn't realized that my mother and father had a matching set, stupid stickers and all! It was embarrassing to see how they stood out in the crowd.

"Please take your seats and place your suitcases on the table in front of you," Miss Miller instructed.

She walked to a small table in the middle of the horseshoe.

"Welcome to your first deportment class," she began.

"What does she mean?" Sam turned to me and whispered.

"I think she means that if we're not good, they'll send us out of the country," I whispered back. But somehow that didn't sound right.

"Since so many of you clearly do not know the meaning of the word *deportment*, I shall take this opportunity to enlighten you," Miss Miller continued. Reading aloud from a large dictionary, she said, "Deportment — the manner in which one conducts oneself or behaves." She put down the dictionary and stared at us. "Of course, for the purposes of these classes, that means *proper* behavior."

"I think I like your definition better, " Sam whispered to me.

"As you know, today's lesson is on how to pack a suitcase," Miss Miller continued.

Mr. Grey started to applaud and then motioned for us to do the same.

"Oh, brother," Sam moaned. "This is ridiculous."

Miss Miller took a little bow and smiled. Then she took a small suitcase from underneath the table. Plaid, of course. Everything Miss Miller owned was plaid. Randy says that she must have been a Scottish bagpiper in another life.

Anyway, that little plaid suitcase was perfectly packed. Obviously I had packed way too many clothes for a two-day trip. I just hoped that she didn't ask us to open up our suitcases.

But no such luck. After Miss Miller did her demonstration, she told us to show what we had packed. Suitcases started popping open all around me — except for mine. I kept jiggling the lock back and forth, but it just wouldn't budge.

Then I noticed that everyone's suitcase was open and they were all watching me. "Please open!" I muttered at the horrible orange monster.

Luckily, Mr. Grey came to my rescue. He shook the suitcase and banged on the lock and it popped open. I was relieved . . . but only for about a second.

Suddenly the cafeteria was filled with this incredibly awful smell. It was almost like one of those toxic accidents you hear about on the news. Except, of course, the smell was a giant bottle of nail polish. Crazy Crimson, to be exact, which was now smeared over most of my clothes!

Frantically I looked through the suitcase for my favorite green-and-white polka-dot socks. I had stuffed the nail polish inside one of them, and somehow the top had come off.

Mr. Grey slowly picked up the sock and held it in the air. Now it was green and white with a gloppy red ball at the toe part where a couple of cotton balls and a Q-tip had stuck to it. It looked like a diseased Christmas decoration.

All the kids were holding their noses and laughing. I just sat there, frozen to my seat. I was so humiliated, I was hoping that the floor would open up and swallow me whole. Without saying a word, Mr. Grey put the sock back in the suitcase and closed the lid. Luckily Miss Miller clapped her hands, motioning for everyone to calm down, or they would have kept laughing forever.

"Miss Wells has just shown us a prime example of the *wrong* way to pack our suitcases," Miss Miller interjected. "Thank you, Miss Wells."

Now I was even more embarrassed and I felt my body blush coming on. But I didn't have time to worry about it, because it was already time for orientation. It was Ms. Nelson's turn, and she explained all the rules and regulations we had to follow while we were on our trip.

We were all going to start out the weekend with one hundred points. Every time we broke one of the rules, five points would be taken off our grade.

We were not allowed to address each other by our first names in public. It had to be either "Miss" or "Mr." Personally, I preferred "Ms." But Ms. Nelson said that twelve-year-old girls were too young to be called "Ms." anything.

As Ms. Nelson spoke, the other teachers loaded us down with pages and pages of summary sheets stating the rules of the trip. I was kind of glad to have it all written down, because there was no way I was going to be able to remember it all! But every time I thought the class was over, they handed us another piece of paper.

One sheet was labeled "Dress Code." Another: "Correct Grammar." Another sheet said "Table Manners," and then there were a whole bunch labeled "Culture Sheets." I finally felt lucky I had such a big suitcase. I would need it to carry all the handouts home!

At last Miss Munson ended the class by saying, "When all else fails, remember, your instructions are to *follow* instructions."

Easy for you to say, Miss Munson, I thought as I dragged my orange suitcase out of the cafeteria. I sighed. It was going to be a very long week.

Just as I suspected, the special classes got harder and harder. By the time Thursday afternoon rolled around, I had so many directions whirling in my head, I didn't know which way was up. But finally our last class, which was called "Proper Attitude," was almost over.

"I hope you have all enjoyed these special classes," Miss Munson said, "and I trust you will conduct yourselves this weekend like ladies and gentlemen."

"Hey, stranger things have happened," Sam whispered to me. "But not much."

I wanted to crack up, but of course I couldn't.

"And don't forget to review your summary sheets," Miss Munson added. At last we were dismissed.

My friends and I left the cafeteria together. We were all secretly thrilled that the classes were over, but we waited until we got outside before we gave a little shout of excitement.

"We made it! No more of those dumb deportment classes!" I exclaimed once we were out in front of the school. "Our weekend has officially begun!"

"Hear! Hear!" Katie and Allison said together.

"I'm with you guys," Randy agreed. "I'm

sure Mr. Hansen feels like he taught us a lesson this week. But I think the worst is over. There's no way they're going to be able to keep score on every single one of those rules and regulations."

"I wouldn't be too sure about that," Katie said.

"I think it's best to be prepared for the worst," Allison added, nodding.

"No way," Randy firmly repeated, her black eyes turning stormy. "There's too many of us, and too few of them. How can they possibly watch everything we do and say for two whole days?"

We all just looked at her for a minute.

"You're probably right," I said doubtfully. But deep in my heart I knew that everyone else was thinking the same thing: *Maybe* they could.

I thought about it all the way home, too. And about packing my suitcase right this time and reading all those summary sheets. Then I decided I would just try my best to remember all the rules and follow instructions. What else could a person do?

On my way home I decided to stop off and get the latest issue of *Young Chic* magazine. I always like to have something to read on a bus trip.

I was about to pay for it when I noticed Mr. Filan, the shopkeeper, putting out a stack of *Hip Teen* magazines. My heart did a flip-flop when I saw a picture of Dylan Palmer on the cover. The headline read: DARING DYLAN DOES THE U.S.A.! TOUR NEWS INSIDE!

I picked up a copy of the magazine and handed some money to Mr. Filan. Then I started to leaf through the pages. At the beginning of the article on Dylan Palmer, I found a brand-new glossy pinup that I didn't have. It was a picture of Dylan standing on a beach with his guitar and one of his horses. I gasped when I saw that he wasn't wearing a shirt. I had never seen a better picture of Dylan. It was perfect for the inside of my locker, to replace the one I had wrinkled up last week.

Dylan used to be a jockey before he got famous, so he's kind of on the short side. That doesn't bother me at all, though, since I'm on the short side, too. I figure that he probably prefers girls that are shorter than he is. And that means I'm just the perfect height.

I kept staring at Dylan's picture. He looked like such a hunk, I thought I was going to die right there on the spot.

He's got long brown hair, green eyes, and this crooked kind of smile. I think it's that crooked smile that really gets to me. And when he talks with that dreamy English accent of his, I just go wild.

"Sabrina . . ." I heard Mr. Filan say. "Are you okay?" he asked, gently calling me back to reality.

"Oh, I'm fine, Mr. Filan," I assured him. "I . . . was just . . ." My voice trailed off again. I just couldn't stop looking at Dylan and thinking about how Stacy Hansen was going to the concert instead of me.

"Well, I know he's the hottest thing in music today," Mr. Filan said, "but is he really worth forgetting two dollars' change?"

I just stared up at Mr. Filan and put my hand out. "You're welcome," I muttered as I left the store in a daze.

I continued flipping through the magazine as I walked down the block. Suddenly I spotted the news that would change my entire life forever. It was right there on page 23. I practically flew all the way home. I had to call Katie right away!

Chapter Four

Sabrina calls Katie.

KATIE: Hello. Beauvais residence. Katie speaking.

SABRINA: Katie! It's me, Sabs! And you're not going to believe what I just found out!

KATIE: What is it?

SABRINA: Guess who's going to be staying at Oak Park Hotel while we're there. Just guess!

KATIE: I don't know. Is it someone we know?

SABRINA: It's definitely someone we want to meet! And he's only going to be in Minneapolis for one weekend!

KATIE: Sabs! You don't mean . . . Dylan Palmer is staying at the Oak Park!?

SABRINA: Yes! Yes! Can you believe it!

KATIE: Ohmygosh! Are you sure? We're

40

	going to be in the same hotel as . . .
SABRINA:	. . . as Dylan Palmer! I just found the schedule for his tour in the new issue of *Hip Teen* magazine. Katie, we'll be right there, in the same place, breathing the same air, and . . .
KATIE:	Yeah, and Stacy Hansen and company will still be the only ones going to the concert. Front row, center, remember? We probably won't even see him.
SABRINA:	No way! There's no way I'm going to get that close to the absolute love of my life and not even see him.
KATIE:	Sabs, didn't you tell me that Dylan travels with his own bodyguards? How are you going to get close to him?
SABRINA:	I don't know. But there's got to be a way, Katie. I'll come up with something. You'll see. Listen, I'm going to call Randy and Al and tell them, too. I'll see you tomorrow.
KATIE:	Okay, Sabs. Bye.
SABRINA:	Bye.

Sabrina calls Randy.

RANDY: Thank you for calling the Zak resi-
            dence. This is Miss Randy Zak.
            May I help you?

SABRINA: Randy? Is that you?

RANDY: (*Laughing*) Yeah, Sabs, it's me. I was
            just practicing the correct way to
            answer the phone.

SABRINA: Oh! For a minute I thought I'd
            dialed the wrong number! Randy,
            wait till you hear this! I've got the
            most incredible news!

RANDY: What is it?

SABRINA: Dylan Palmer is staying at the Oak
            Park this weekend! Can you believe
            it?

RANDY: Totally rad! What a coincidence!

SABRINA: Isn't it wild? I just know we'll get to
            meet him. I can feel it!

RANDY: I don't know, Sabs. Big rock 'n' roll
            stars always have crowds of securi-
            ty people around them to keep the
            fans away. My dad says it's almost
            impossible to get through them,
            too.

SABRINA: I know, I know. But I absolutely have to meet him!

RANDY: You know, Sabs, I asked my father if he could get us tickets to Dylan's concert.

SABRINA: You did? Why didn't you tell me? Did he get the tickets?

RANDY: I didn't tell you 'cause I wasn't sure he would be able to get them. I didn't want to get your hopes up. I spoke to him about it over the phone, but he's on a job in France and couldn't do anything from there. Sorry.

SABRINA: Well, thanks for trying. At least we'll be able to say that we stayed in the same hotel as Dylan Palmer!

RANDY: Cool! Hey, I've got to tell M to stop working so she can eat some dinner. I'll talk to you tomorrow, okay?

SABRINA: Sure. I have to call Allison, anyway, and I've still got packing to do. Bye, Ran.

RANDY: *Ciao.*

Sabrina calls Allison.

ALLISON: Hello?

SABRINA: Hi, Al. It's me, Sabrina.

ALLISON: I'm glad you called. I have some news for you.

SABRINA: Really? I have some news for you, too . . . but you go first.

ALLISON: Okay — well, I know you haven't finished reading the summary sheets yet, so I just thought I'd let you know about this before we left.

SABRINA: About what?

ALLISON: In the packet there's a brochure about our hotel. On the bottom of page two it says, "Albert Hansen, manager of the Oak Park Hotel, will be happy to assist you."

SABRINA: So? Who's Albert . . . HANSEN!? Oh, no!

ALLISON: Oh, yes! Remember how many times Stacy's bragged about her bigshot uncle who's in the hotel business?

SABRINA: So that's how she got those tickets!

ALLISON: What? I don't understand.

SABRINA: Well, *my* news is that Dylan Palmer is staying at the Oak Park, too!

ALLISON: Wow! So you think Stacy got the tickets from her uncle, who got them from Dylan?

SABRINA: Right! She's such a sneak!

ALLISON: I know what you mean.

SABRINA: Oh, well. If we can't have tickets to the concert, at least we'll be able to see Dylan in our hotel.

ALLISON: And who knows what might happen when we do see him, Sabs.

SABRINA: Yeah! I'd better start reading those summary sheets now, though. Otherwise I probably won't make it all the way to Minneapolis!

ALLISON: See you tomorrow, Sabs.

SABRINA: Bye, Al.

Chapter Five

After dinner I had a lot to do to get ready for the trip. I started by packing my suitcase. I had to admit it was much easier packing this time, after Miss Miller's class. Then I had to wash my hair and polish my nails. I wanted to look my best for my weekend in the big city.

Besides, you never know *who* you might run into at a fancy hotel like the Oak Park.

Last on my list was that pile of dumb summary sheets. I tried to start reading them as my nail polish dried. But I knew I just wasn't concentrating. I was too excited about the trip. And I had to spend some time figuring out what to do about Dylan.

I knew it was crazy, but I decided to read through every magazine article I had on Dylan Palmer. I knew just about every word of them by heart, but I was hoping that looking through them all again might help me come up with some kind of plan.

I had tons of information, and I kept it all in three huge clear plastic boxes my dad had brought home from his hardware store. Two were filled with magazine and newspaper clippings, and the other held piles and piles of pictures.

That's the thing that got to me so much. I just knew I was the biggest Dylan Palmer fan in the whole world. I belonged to his international fan club and wrote him a fan letter at least once a week. I was sure Stacy didn't know half as much about him as I did. It just wasn't fair that she had those front-row tickets and I didn't have any.

Those summary sheets were starting to bug me. I was just so involved with trying to figure out how to meet Dylan, I kept putting off reading them. I was pretty sure we had covered it all in class, anyway.

It was pretty late when I finally decided that there was nothing more I could do to prepare. I put on my headphones and played my favorite Dylan Palmer song, "I'll Be True Blue to You." It wasn't exactly Dylan's most famous rock song, but I liked it best because he talked in the middle of it. I just knew his dreamy voice would lull me off to sleep. And it did!

Amazingly I got up early the next morning and made it to school on time. That's what happens when I'm really excited about something. We only had classes for half a day. Then we were allowed to go home to change and get our suitcases. The buses would leave from the school parking lot at two o'clock.

It was a long morning. Most of us spent the entire time watching the clock. We just couldn't wait for that last bell to ring.

When it did, I practically flew home to change my clothes and get my stuff. My mom had bought a set of wheels that strapped on the bottom of my suitcase, so at least the orange monster was easier to handle.

"Wow, Sabs! You've been on time twice in one day," Randy commented as we stood in front of the school waiting for the buses to arrive. "I wonder where Al and Katie are?"

"That's weird," I said, peering down the street. "I hope they don't miss the bus."

"No way," Katie said from behind me, tapping my shoulder. "We're here!"

"And I got a new watch, just to make sure none of us get any points taken off for not being punctual." Allison beamed as she held out her wrist to show it off.

"Wow, that's cool," Randy said as she looked at Allison's watch. "Look, it's even got an alarm on it!"

But as I moved closer to see it, I couldn't help but notice the strange way Katie and Al were looking at me and Randy.

"How come you're not dressed?" Katie asked a few seconds later.

"What do you mean?" I looked down at my outfit. I was wearing gold leggings, a matching striped oversized T-shirt, white running shoes, and a white sweatshirt tied around my shoulders. It wasn't my best outfit, but I thought I looked pretty good.

"I wanted to be comfortable on the bus." I shrugged, eyeing Katie's navy blue suit. She was also wearing a white blouse, navy blue leather flats, and pearl earrings.

"Sabrina, didn't you read those summary sheets last night?" Allison asked as she adjusted her burgundy skirt. She was wearing a matching jacket with a black velvet collar, plus a white blouse and black leather flats. She had a black velvet ribbon weaved through her braid. Like the rest of us, she was also carrying her coat.

"Where are your little white gloves, Al?" Randy joked as she spun around to model her black jumpsuit. Underneath it she wore a purple long-sleeved shirt with big round black buttons. She also wore black half boots and a funky black derby with a red hatband. "Whoops! I forgot mine, too!" She giggled, spreading out her fingers in front of her face.

Suddenly I got really nervous. I looked around and noticed that Randy and I and a couple of other kids were definitely underdressed. Arizonna looked like he was ready to go to the beach.

"Sabs, didn't you read the summary sheets?" Katie asked softly.

"Uh, I did kind of look them over. But I guess I missed the one on the dress code," I stammered. "What did it say?"

"No pants, for one thing," Al said as she and Katie stared at me in disbelief.

"Oh, no . . . what else?" I asked again, almost afraid to hear the answer.

Katie hesitated for a moment. "Well, we're not supposed to wear jeans. We have to have a sweater or a jacket; no bare shoulders. And we can only wear clear nail polish."

I looked down at my gold polish. I had found this really cool yellow-gold neon polish that matched my leggings exactly. I hoped that one of the girls had brought along some nail polish remover.

"No hanging earrings," Allison continued, looking at the silver stars hanging from Randy's ears. "No sneakers, and no boots."

"Girls have to carry a purse. Boys have to wear a shirt and tie," Katie added in a gloomy voice.

I spun my head around to try and find Sam. He was hanging out with Billy Dixon, Jason McKee, and Arizonna Blake. I was so busy thinking about Dylan Palmer, I hadn't even noticed that Sam had gotten all decked out in a blue shirt and a tie. I couldn't believe he was taking this all so seriously.

"Randy, did you read all this stuff?" I yelped, shooting a look at Randy.

"Nope!" she replied. "I went to those dumb classes and that was enough. Besides, I *like* the way *I* dress!" she answered defiantly.

Just then we all saw Miss Miller heading toward us. She was wearing a green tartan plaid suit and a plaid hat that had a little green feather sticking out of the hatband. She looked like she had a plaid bird on her head.

"Ladies and gentlemen," she sang out. "Time to line up! Alphabetical order, please. Take your places! The buses will be arriving momentarily."

We all looked at one another and shrugged.

"Well, I guess this is good-bye," I said.

"It's a good thing they're going to allow us to room together," Katie added. "Or else we'd never get to see each other!"

"Come on, come on," Miss Miller continued, clapping her hands together.

Reluctantly we all did as we were told.

"Well, at least we get to sit together," Sam commented as he took his place in line behind me.

"No talking," Miss Munson said as she motioned us all into place. "We've got a lot of work to do. Please line up your suitcases, displaying your I.D. tags."

Oh, no! I thought to myself. I forgot to get an I.D. tag! I elbowed Sam.

"Hey — stop jabbing me, Sabs!" he mumbled under his breath.

"Do you have another I.D. tag?" I whispered.

"I forgot mine."

"No," he shot back in a hushed whisper. "Now, cut it out, Sabs, or we'll get points taken off. . . ."

Just then I noticed Mr. Grey working his way down the line. He was carrying a huge clipboard. My stomach started to get all fluttery.

"Mr. Samuel Wells," he said without lifting his head from the board.

"Present and accounted for," Sam said, practically clicking his heels together.

I couldn't help but gasp in disbelief. Sam was acting like he was in the army or something.

"Pass," Mr. Grey said with a smile. "Good work, Mr. Wells."

"Thank you, sir . . . er . . . Mr. Grey." Sam saluted.

"Miss Sabrina Wells," Mr. Grey said, smiling at me. Then he looked down at my suitcase. "No I.D. tags, Miss Wells?" he questioned as he lifted the suitcase and turned it around.

It was awfully weird having him call me "Miss Wells" like that. I could feel my face burning up.

"Uh . . . no. Sorry, Mr. Grey," I added as I watched him put a mark down next to my name.

Then he stood back and eyed my outfit.

"I'm sorry, too, Miss Wells," he said, puckering up his lips. "But you know I'll have to mark you down for ten points total."

"Ten points?" I asked in disbelief. "I thought it was only five!"

"Five for mislabeling of personal property, and five for grooming. Your outfit doesn't meet trip standards," he said, making another mark on his clipboard.

I took a deep breath as I felt my chin starting to quiver. We weren't even on the bus yet and I already had ten points taken off my grade! This certainly didn't look good for a class president. So much for Randy's prediction that the teachers wouldn't keep score on all these rules.

"Sorry, Mr. Grey," I repeated as I felt myself straightening up. "I'll try to do better."

"That's the spirit, Miss Wells," he said with a smile. "The trip has just begun. You have plenty of time for improvement."

I held my breath as I watched Mr. Grey check the girl in front of me. As soon as he moved on, I sat down on my suitcase and heaved a deep sigh.

Luckily I had the summary sheets with me,

and I could read them on the bus. My plan for meeting Dylan Palmer would have to wait.

Obviously this trip was going to be serious business.

Chapter Six

"If we have to go through this every time we line up, this trip is going to take a billion years," Sam whispered to me.

"Tell me about it," I whispered back. "And where are the buses?" I added, stretching out my neck to look.

"Miss Wells, stay in line!" Ms. Nelson called.

"Wow. This is like being in prison," I muttered under my breath.

"I don't think prisoners get to travel first class," Sam shot back, and motioned to the red-and-tan tour buses pulling up to the curb.

"Excellent!" Sam gasped as he looked down the line to check out Jason's and Billy's reactions.

I just stood there staring at the huge red and gold letters printed across the side of the bus. They said PRINCESS MOTOR LINES. On the bottom, in smaller letters, it said FOR THE ROYAL TREATMENT.

This was totally awesome! Mr. Grey, Ms. Nelson, Miss Miller, and Miss Munson all lined up at the front of the first bus. Then the doors opened automatically and two uniformed drivers stepped out of the bus. They were both tall and handsome. They were wearing blue suits and caps with gold braid across the brims and looked more like airplane pilots than bus drivers. Katie glanced at me from her place on the line and flashed an approving smile.

Then all the teachers and the drivers shook hands. This was definitely not going to be a typical field trip. It looked more like a reception line at the White House!

Usually, when we go on a class trip, we end up on some rickety yellow school bus with a driver named Mac or something. And he's always dressed like a construction worker or a plumber.

I watched as our two drivers opened up two large doors on the side of the bus.

"Our drivers will load the luggage. Please wait for their signal to board the bus," Ms. Nelson said.

"Boy, this really is first class," I whispered to Sam.

"A little different from our camping trips, eh, Sabs?" he whispered back.

"A *little*," I joked back. With such a big family, we hardly ever went on fancy trips. But Sam and I were sure making up for that now.

Just then pilot number one smiled and motioned us forward. Sam and I handed him our luggage and climbed aboard the bus. I thought it was totally awesome that I got a window seat on the first bus. Sam and I usually fight over it, but our instructions were to take the first available seat, so he couldn't do anything about it.

Unfortunately, I ended up sitting right across the aisle from Stacy. I just knew this was going to be a long trip. I hated not being with my friends. But at least Sam was sitting between us.

"Only twenty-nine more hours to Dylan," Stacy said loud enough for everyone to hear.

The words were like a knife cutting through my heart. My friends and I had hardly had a chance to talk about our plan. In fact, we didn't even have a real plan!

"So, what are you wearing to the concert?" B.Z. asked Stacy as the teachers started boarding the bus.

"I bought a new outfit from Dare," Stacy

replied, pulling out her mirror to inspect her makeup. "It's a peach-striped jumpsuit," she babbled as she applied an extra coat of mascara to her already clumpy lashes.

Good! I thought to myself. I happened to know that Dylan detested stripes and pastel colors. One of the articles in my file said he loved bold colors on women. Stacy usually wore pastel colors. She really had an awesome wardrobe, but most of her clothes made her look like a walking ice-cream cone. But what was the difference? She was going to see Dylan in concert, and I wasn't. It was still bugging me, I guess. Then Miss Munson's shrill voice cut through my thoughts.

"Mr. Grey!" she screeched. "Five points for Miss Hansen!"

"*Me?* What did I do?" Stacy squealed. She just couldn't believe that her totally perfect self could possibly do anything wrong.

"Mr. Grey!" Miss Munson screeched even louder. "Make that fifteen points!"

"*What?. . . I . . .*" Stacy began, standing up quickly.

"Sit down, Miss Hansen," Miss Munson demanded. "That's five points for talking loudly in public, five points for answering back to a teacher, and five points for applying makeup in a public place. That's what a ladies' room is for," she said, putting the emphasis on the word *ladies*.

"You can't take some people anywhere," I whispered as soon as Miss Munson was out of earshot. I didn't even bother to check out Stacy's reaction. I just looked out the window, smiling to myself.

I settled into my seat and relaxed. It was so plush, it felt more comfortable than our living room sofa.

"Hey, Sabs, this is pretty cool, huh?" Sam commented as he sat up in his seat. Then he started fiddling with the handles on his armrest.

"What are those for?" I asked, looking over to see if there were any on my side. But just as I said it, the back of Sam's seat flipped back and his head landed right on top of Miss Miller's plaid lap!

He smiled his nervous smile. "Hi, Miss Miller! Just decided to drop in for a little chat," he joked.

Everyone around us started to giggle.

Miss Miller looked down at Sam and scowled. Her nose was so close to his, they were practically touching.

"FIVE POINTS, Mr. Wells!" she boomed in a loud voice. "Did you hear that, Mr. Grey?" she said without turning her head. "That's five points for Mr. Wells."

Then she flipped the handle back. Sam's chair shot up so fast he hit his head against the headrest.

Everybody was trying to stop laughing. But Sam looked so funny, all we could do was lower our heads and try to muffle our giggles.

"Man!" Sam griped as he sat up. "I'm going to sue her for whiplash," he moaned, rubbing his neck.

"You'd better calm down, Sam," I whispered as the driver started the motor. "I bet they'll leave us alone in a few minutes, anyway."

Sam just shot me his don't-count-on-it look, loosened his tie, and angrily sat back in his seat.

I dug into my purse and pulled out my summary sheets. But the second I found them, pilot number two stood up at the front of the bus and pulled a microphone down from the ceiling.

"Ladies and gentlemen," he began, "welcome to Princess Motor Lines tours. My name is Robert, and I will be your tour guide."

"I was wondering why we had two drivers," I

whispered to Sam.

"Wow! A driver and a tour guide. Awesome! But why do we need him here now?" Sam questioned. "We won't be in Minneapolis for another couple of hours."

"Right now," Robert continued, "I would like to introduce you to your driver, Alex."

Alex gave us a wave without taking his eyes off the road. I could see his face in his big rearview mirror. He had a big smile on his face. I had to admit, I couldn't help smiling myself with all these cheerful people around!

"Now, I'll bet you all have a lot of questions about the city, don't you?" Robert asked.

We all just kind of nodded. I think we were afraid to talk.

"But I'll bet you didn't realize that you are the ones who will be answering all those questions — before we even get there," he said, laughing.

Everyone started squirming in their seats. I was beginning to think this bus ride wasn't going to be much fun after all.

"So, at this time, I'm going to be turning the microphone over to your teacher, Ms. Nelson, and she's going to tell you all about the wonderful things we have in store for you. I'll check back with you in a few minutes," he said with a wink.

We all remained quiet as Ms. Nelson smiled and took the microphone. Suddenly I didn't feel like smiling anymore.

"Good afternoon, ladies and gentle —" she began. Abruptly she stopped talking and put down the microphone. All eyes were upon her as she walked to the back of the bus.

"Mr. Grey," she called out. "Five points for Miss Zak," she calmly said, and removed a set of headphones from Randy's ears.

"Huh! Wha'?" Randy mumbled as if someone had just woken her up from a nap.

"No personal radios!" Ms. Nelson announced, and went back to the front of the bus.

As I looked back toward where Randy was sitting, I saw Katie and Allison looking at me from the other side of the aisle. Then they both turned around and looked at Randy, too.

Randy just shrugged her shoulders as if to say, "So what." Then she crossed her arms and sat back in her seat.

"As I was saying," Ms. Nelson continued, "the first topic on our agenda is Cultural Enrichment . . . ." She paused again and walked to the back of the bus.

"Mr. Grey," she called in the same tone of voice as the first time. "Five points for Miss Zak," she repeated as she tapped her foot and held out a tissue in the palm of her hand.

Randy reached in her mouth and pulled out a huge wad of bubble gum.

"No gum," Ms. Nelson announced, walking back to the front of the bus.

Randy just raised her eyebrows. It looked like she was finally getting the message. Our teachers were really serious about teaching us manners.

We all straightened up in our seats as Ms. Nelson took the microphone for the third time. A few seconds later I slowly turned around and got Randy's attention.

She put up her hands as if to say, "What are we gonna do?"

I turned back to the front of the bus.

"Please take out your culture sheets," Ms. Nelson said. As I fumbled through the pile of papers in my lap, Miss Miller walked down the aisle of seats, handing out brand-new softcover books that said *Touring Minneapolis* on the front.

Finally I found the culture sheets at the bottom of the stack. There were three of them. Each one had about fifteen questions on it. We were supposed to find the answers to the questions in our tour books.

"Why don't they just call this an open-book quiz?" Sam mumbled, pulling a pencil from his pocket.

"They told us this trip wasn't going to be for fun and pleasure," I reminded him, opening my tour book.

After about ten minutes I looked up from my tour book. The bus was really quiet. I looked over at Allison and Katie, but they didn't notice me. They were both busily reading their tour books and filling out their sheets. Practicing perfect deportment, you might say.

I gazed around the bus again and luckily caught Randy's eye. I mouthed out the words, "How many points?"

Her black eyes widened as she held up five fingers. Then she flashed another five. That was ten. Not too bad. But then she flashed her fingers three more times! Twenty-five points! I couldn't believe it.

I only had ten and I was freaking out. Sam had five. But Randy had racked up twenty-five big ones! And we hadn't even reached Minneapolis yet!

Chapter Seven

"Welcome to Minneapolis," Robert sang out as our bus approached the city. "Whether you prefer great theater at the award-winning Guthrie, or just strolling along Minneapolis's cobblestoned Main Street riverfront, there's something for everyone in Minneapolis!"

Now I was kind of glad we had done those culture sheets. After spending the last hour reading about all these different places, it was really exciting to actually see them in person.

"History comes alive at Fort Snelling and historic Murphy's Landing, where the 1800s are recreated with authenticity and excitement," Robert went on. He sounded like a robot tour guide from outer space.

"Before we go to your hotel, we're going to take a minitour of the town, just to show you some of the highlights."

I sat up in my seat to get the best view. We

passed the Minneapolis Planetarium, and the Ard Godfrey House, which was supposed to be the oldest house in the city.

I hoped we'd get a chance to go inside. I thought it would be neat to walk through a house that was built in 1849, and there's supposed to be this cradle there where the first pioneer baby girl born in Minneapolis slept.

We drove by the Minneapolis Institute of Arts, which Robert said was one of the greatest museums in America. There had been plenty of questions about it on our culture sheet, so I guessed we were going to spend a lot of time in there.

I looked around the bus. Everyone either had their necks stretched out, trying to check out what was on the other side of the bus, or they had their noses pressed against the windows. There was so much to look at, it was hard to stay in our seats. I was sorry that we weren't allowed to take pictures while we were on the bus. But Ms. Nelson wouldn't allow it. She said it was because we were supposed to stay in our seats.

I looked at Allison. She was scribbling notes in the margins of her tour book as we passed each of the sights on our tour. Katie couldn't seem to take her eyes off the city. Even Randy seemed to be psyched now.

"Hey, there's the Metrodome on the right," Billy called out as we passed the huge domed sports center. I turned around in my seat to look where he was pointing. The Metrodome was where the Dylan Palmer concert was going to be held. It certainly was a lot bigger than the Bradley Band Shell. That's where we hold all our concerts in Acorn Falls.

"Eeee!" Stacy, Eva, B.Z., and Laurel screamed. "Dylan Palmer, HERE WE COME!" they cheered.

"Mr. Grey!" Miss Munson called out. "Five MORE points for Miss Hansen, Miss Malone, Miss Latimer, and Miss Spencer!"

That really shut them up fast. But even though they were getting points taken off, I still got that queasy feeling in my stomach again. I just had to think of a way to meet Dylan Palmer!

Then Sam suddenly called out, "All right!" and I spun around to see what he was so excited about.

"Totally radical! Hey, Sabs, look at that!" he shouted, pointing out the window. "That's the weirdest thing I've ever seen!"

"Totally," Arizonna agreed. The bus slowed

down to pass the Minneapolis Sculpture Garden and we all stood up to get a good look.

"Mr. Grey, five points for Mr. Wells and Miss Wells, and Mr. Blake," Miss Munson snapped.

The Sculpture Garden was like a big park with all these huge art pieces scattered on the grass. In the middle there was a giant gray spoon with a giant red cherry sitting in it.

It really was an awesome sight. The whole bus was buzzing with comments. Even the teachers were excited. No one was telling us to be quiet anymore.

"Hey! There's water coming out of it," Sam shouted. He twisted in his seat to get a better look.

"That must be the Spoonbridge and Cherry fountain!" Miss Miller said. I hurriedly looked up the picture in my tour book.

"It is!" I confirmed. "And it says here that the Minneapolis Sculpture Garden is the biggest urban sculpture garden in the whole world," I read out loud.

"How would you like to eat your cornflakes out of that!" Greg Loggins joked.

I guess that was because we all had our tour books out, and we were looking up practically every attraction we saw. It was so cool to finally be in Minneapolis after all those weeks of talking about it and thinking about it. I could feel the energy of the city from inside the bus.

"There's hardly any room for people on the street," Katie commented as we watched everyone squashing against one another on the sidewalks. We seemed to be right in the middle of rush hour.

"New York's even worse that this," Randy told us. "But it's pretty intense out there, too!"

"Ladies and gentlemen, please put your tour books away now," Robert called from the front of the bus. "We'll be arriving at the Oak Park Hotel momentarily, and we'll need to proceed in an orderly fashion."

Just hearing the words *Oak Park Hotel* made me feel like my heart was going to jump right out of my body. My thoughts turned to Dylan again. Maybe he'd be standing outside or maybe in the lobby. No, that's ridiculous, I told myself. If a big rock star like Dylan Palmer just walked around in public like a normal person, he'd be mobbed in a second.

"Ladies and gentlemen, calm down," Ms.

Nelson warned us. "Please follow instructions and don't forget your manners!"

Once she said that, we all quieted down. It wasn't that we were really worried about manners. It was just that we didn't want any more points taken off our grades.

Before I knew it, we were driving through the hotel district. I've never seen so many hotels in one place. All we have in Acorn Falls is one little motel, the Acorn Motor Lodge.

Finally we drove up to a large brown brick building. I could tell right away from the picture in my tour book that it was the Oak Park.

The first thing I recognized was the long green canopy. It was edged with a gold scallop design. When the sun hit it, it glistened so much, it looked like it was moving.

Above the canopy was a green-and-tan sign that read THE OAK PARK. It was written in gold-script lettering and there were two huge gold oak leaves on either side of the name. It was so posh, it gave me butterflies in my stomach.

Underneath the canopy there was a red carpet that stretched all the way out to the curb. All along the carpet there were big potted plants. The red carpet looked like it was a mile long. The minute I saw it, I thought of the Academy Awards. I always love to watch the stars coming in at the beginning of the show, walking along that long red carpet. When I walked up the carpet into the Oak Park, I knew I would feel like I was almost a real star, too.

At the entrance to the hotel, there was a huge door with three gigantic gold pillars on each side. Two doormen were standing on the sidewalk in front of the canopy, at the curb. They tipped their hats as soon as they saw the bus pull up in front of the hotel. My first impulse was to wave back. But Miss Miller was staring right at me and I was afraid she might take some points off my score for unauthorized waving.

Alex and Robert stepped out first, and then all our teachers got off. We watched as everyone shook hands with the doormen.

I was so happy to have arrived at last, I wanted just to jump off the bus and run into the lobby. I think everyone else did, too. After all, we had done that on all our other school trips.

But this trip was different. We were all so afraid of getting points marked against us, we just sat in our seats and waited for instructions. It seemed to take forever.

At last Ms. Nelson and Mr. Grey boarded the bus. Sam sat up and hurriedly adjusted his tie.

"Ladies and gentlemen, Alex and Robert will now unload your luggage and it will be lined up along that red carpet beneath the canopy," Ms. Nelson announced. "After you have identified your bag, we'll meet in the lobby, where you'll receive your room assignments and keys. You'll have approximately ninety minutes to get ready for dinner in the hotel dining room, which will be followed by our trip to the theater. We'll meet in the lobby at six-thirty sharp for dinner. Don't forget to take all your personal belongings," she called back as Alex assisted her off the bus.

I wasn't sure if that meant we were supposed to take our own luggage or not. So I just decided to wait and see what everybody else did.

"Don't worry about lining up in alphabetical order," Mr. Grey kept repeating as we stepped out onto the sidewalk. "As soon as you find your luggage, just proceed."

I was trying to figure out what "just proceed" meant when I saw the next bus pulling up behind us. Alex immediately got back onto our bus and pulled it up a couple of yards.

Within seconds the rest of the seventh grade

was standing in front of the Oak Park. I searched for one of my friends, but I couldn't find any of them in the crowd. Finally I gave up.

I looked at the luggage lined up along the red carpet. There seemed to be a million suitcases!

But it wasn't hard to find my orange monster. It was the last one in the row, closest to the sidewalk. I had thought the strap-on wheels were going to make my suitcase look more up-to-date and easier to handle. But the wheels were too tiny for the case, and the straps that attached them were really thick and bright yellow. So now my suitcase looked even worse next to the ones everyone else had. Horrified, I noticed a doorman moving in on it. I rushed over, too, and we reached it at the very same moment.

"Oh! That's mine," I called out.

"I'm sorry, miss," he apologized. "But I'm afraid the tags have been lost."

The last thing I wanted to do was draw any attention to myself. Suddenly the only thing that seemed important was getting that orange horror out of sight.

"Oh, I'm *positive* this one's mine," I assured

him as I reached for the handle.

"Allow me," he replied, trying to pry the handle from my grip.

"No, please. I'll take care of it," I argued, tugging it away from him. "Thank you," I said, giving the suitcase a little shove onto the long red carpet.

But I lost my grip, and before I knew what was happening, the tiny little wheels spun into action. I watched in horror as the suitcase careened along the red carpet all by itself. It swerved and swayed, narrowly missing one of the potted plants like a hot rod in the Demolition Derby. People exiting the hotel were desperately trying to jump out of its way.

"Wait! Come back!" I called out as I chased after my runaway suitcase. But just as I started to catch up, the rubber of my sneaker got caught on the rug and I fell flat on my face.

Immediately an army of doormen and bellhops came to my rescue. When I got back on my feet, I was just in time to see my suitcase crash into one of the gold pillars. It bounced back from the pillar, wobbled for a moment, then fell on its side and popped open. My clothes spilled out in every direction.

Exhausted, I looked up to find Mr. Grey standing beside me.

"I know, I know," I mumbled sadly. "Five points, for not following directions."

Chapter Eight

Minutes later Katie, Randy, Al, and I were all sitting in the ladies' room attending to my wounds. Not that I was really hurt, or anything like that. I just had a small bruise on my cheek, and my hands were filthy. Basically I was totally embarrassed.

"All he said was 'Just proceed,' " I argued as Katie placed a damp paper towel on my forehead.

"You're right," Randy said, washing her hands in the magnificent pink-and-silver sink. "The directions weren't very clear. I bet you could fight them on that one, Sabs."

"I think you should consider yourself lucky," Katie cut in.

"*Lucky!*" I shot back, staring at myself in the ornate gold mirror. "Look at me! I'm a mess!"

"I think what Katie means is you're lucky you didn't get more than five points taken off," Allison concluded.

"Al's right," Randy agreed. "I'm surprised Mr. Grey didn't pack you up and ship you back to Acorn Falls right inside your runaway suitcase!"

"Yeah. It gets a lot more miles per gallon than the bus," Katie chimed in, keeping a straight face.

I looked at my friends, wondering if they were serious or not. For a second there, I was feeling kind of hurt. But then Katie burst out laughing, and we all cracked up.

Suddenly we heard this tiny beeping sound coming from Allison's wrist.

"Oh! That's my alarm," she proudly announced. "Good! This didn't put us off schedule."

"Oh, brother," I moaned. "You mean, you're going to use that thing to keep us on schedule for the whole trip!"

"Well, I set it ten minutes fast. That way we'll never be late for anything."

"I think it's a great idea," Katie said, gathering up the crumpled paper towels and tossing them into the trash can.

"Me too," Randy agreed, grabbing her purse. "We'd better get out of here. We don't have much time to get settled and eat before we have to leave for the play."

"And we haven't even gotten our room assignments yet!" Allison added. "Let's motor!"

We all trooped out to the lobby. I wasn't too thrilled at the thought of facing the other kids. Luckily, by the time we got to the desk, it looked like most of our class was already gone.

"Is everything under control?" Mr. Grey asked, inspecting my cheek. Just having him that close to me made my heart flutter. I'm always trying to get Mr. Grey to notice me. But on this trip I was getting a lot more attention than I had bargained for — and not exactly the right kind, either.

"Yes, thank you, Mr. Grey," I responded politely.

"Then please take a seat over there," he instructed, pointing to a huge gold circular couch. "Mr. Hansen will be with you in a moment."

For a moment I was a little confused. Mr. Hansen hadn't even come on the trip! But then I realized he must be talking about Stacy's uncle Albert.

We walked over to the couch. I really wanted

to roam around and look at all the fancy furniture and decorations, but I didn't want to take any more chances. I decided just to sit down and look from there.

When I had first walked into the lobby, I was so shaken up that I hadn't noticed anything. But now that I felt calmer, I had a chance to look at everything.

The lobby was decorated in peach, green, and cream. There were gold mirrors and crystal chandeliers everywhere you looked. It was very sophisticated.

The carpet was really neat. I had never seen one quite like it. It was sort of an apple green with peach accents, and it had three different patterns on it. In some places there was a diamond pattern, in other places it turned into stripes, and then there were little boxes filled with gold rosebuds all around the edge. I couldn't picture something so confusing in our house, but it looked beautiful in the hotel.

"Look at how high the ceiling is!" Katie gasped in amazement.

I looked up. All around the border at the top of the walls there were dancing angels, pretty birds, and flowers with huge golden leaves. I decided that golden leaves must be some kind of theme at the Oak Park. They seemed to be everywhere. The ceiling kind of reminded me of what heaven was supposed to look like.

"That must all be hand-painted," Allison said, tilting her head back.

"Definitely," Randy agreed, doing the same.

"If you're not careful, one of those birds might land one right in your eye," I heard a familiar voice quip.

"Shut up, Sam" I said without even looking.

"Suit yourself, bird-watchers," Nick Robbins answered matter-of-factly. "But Mr. Hansen has called for Miss Zak two times already," he told us as they walked off toward the elevator.

We all scrambled to our feet and made a mad dash for the desk.

"Here! Here!" Katie said, reaching the desk before the rest of us.

I was amazed at how much this Mr. Hansen looked like our Mr. Hansen. You could tell they were brothers. They looked like twins. Even their bald spots were in the same place.

"Your party?" Mr. Albert Hansen asked.

"Zak," Randy answered promptly.

"Welcome to the Oak Park," he said, putting

on this fake smile.

"He is definitely Stacy's uncle," Katie whispered to me.

"Totally," I agreed. Stacy's uncle smiled the same way Stacy always did.

"Miss Rowena Zak and company," Mr. Hansen muttered as he looked down the list.

I stole a glance at Randy just as she started to scowl. There's nothing Randy hates more than being called Rowena. But this trip was so formal, they had made us use our full names for everything.

We were supposed to use one name for each room reservation, and we had all agreed it should be Randy's because it was the shortest.

"Miss Cloud, Miss Campbell, and Miss Wells. Correct?" Mr. Hansen asked snootily, looking down at us.

"Correct." We all nodded.

As he was searching for our keys, I noticed the huge wall of message boxes on the wall behind him. There must have been hundreds of them. Each one had a number underneath it.

Too bad they don't have names, I thought. That way I could have found out which room Dylan was staying in.

I looked around. Everything seemed so quiet and normal. You'd never guess that somewhere in this building there was a famous rock star. I was starting to wonder if Dylan Palmer was really staying here after all.

Just as I was thinking that, Stacy and her gang came strutting through the lobby.

"Better late than never," B.Z. loudly quipped to Laurel Spencer, looking toward us. "They must be the last ones."

"Stacy and her friends sure have been talking loudly this trip," Randy commented with a smirk on her face.

"Maybe they're all going deaf." Katie giggled.

I wasn't even paying attention. I was watching Mr. Hansen look over his list again. Obviously there was some kind of problem with our room reservation.

"Excuse me for a moment, please, ladies," Mr. Hansen said, and walked over to whisper to Ms. Nelson and Mr. Grey.

"Hi, Uncle Albert," Stacy cooed as she passed us. "Thank you for the big, beautiful room," she added, emphasizing the word *big*.

"Oh, brother," Randy muttered.

But I was too busy watching Mr. Hansen talk

with our teachers. He kept looking over at us in a way that got me worried.

Maybe there were no rooms left. Or maybe they wanted me to pay for the damage my suitcase had done to one of the palm trees out front. As the orange nightmare whizzed by, it had torn off a few leaves. Was that such a big deal? Finally Mr. Hansen and Mr. Grey came over to us.

"Girls, there's been a mixup in the room reservations," Mr. Grey began.

"I do apologize," Mr. Hansen cut in. "But we don't have any more rooms left on the same floor the rest of your class is staying on."

My heart sunk. We all looked at one another.

"What Mr. Hansen wants to do is give you a master suite a few floors above us," Mr. Grey went on.

A master suite! My heart jumped at the thought.

"That's fine," we all agreed, trying to sound casual when we were ready to burst.

"Room twenty-three," Mr. Hansen said with another fake smile. He handed Randy two sets of keys. "Your bags will be coming up shortly," he added.

"Remember your manners, now," Ms. Nelson

reminded us as we headed for the elevators. "Behave like the nice young ladies you are!"

"Yes, Ms. Nelson," Randy assured her, sending her voice in Stacy's direction. "Mr. Hansen did say our suite was on the twentieth floor, didn't he?" she asked, holding up the room keys.

Ms. Nelson nodded. Stacy turned around just in time to see the elevator doors closing in front of us. We were finally alone.

"YES! YES! YES!" I cheered, jumping up and down.

"Be careful," Katie warned me. "This a glass elevator. Everyone can see us."

In my excitement I hadn't even noticed. I looked out. You could look down and see the entire lobby and everyone in it.

"Look at Stacy and Laurel." Randy pointed. "They're getting smaller and smaller."

I looked down. Stacy was standing in the lobby, looking up at us. Even though we were getting farther and farther away, I could still tell that she was fuming.

"She's having a fit," I screeched.

"This will kill her." Randy laughed as she peered down at Stacy, wildly waving the room keys.

"Will you forget about Stacy," Allison said with a smile. "Let's go see our room. I can't wait!"

When the elevator opened on the twentieth floor, we jumped out so quickly, we practically tripped over each other's feet as we ran down the hall.

"There it is!" Katie said, pointing to a door that said "23."

"Let's do this right," Randy teased. She slowly eased the key into the lock.

"Oh, come on!" I pleaded. "Hurry up!"

As soon as she got the door open, we all tumbled in.

"Awesome!" Randy exclaimed.

"This is incredible!" Allison gasped.

"Wow!" Katie and I said at exactly the same time.

Cautiously we all walked around the huge room. Everything in it was a pale golden-yellow color. There were two large golden wingback chairs, a matching sofa, and a long cherrywood coffee table with an enormous vase of red roses sitting in the middle of it.

The wallpaper had a creamy off-white background, with pale yellow oak leaves that felt like they were cut out of velvet. The lamps were brass.

"This is unbelievable," I gasped, looking around. "But where are we supposed to sleep?"

"He told us we had a master suite," Randy pointed out as she opened a set of doors on one side of the room. "This is just the sitting area. The bedrooms are inside!"

"I'm sleeping in the pink room!" Katie called, running over to the gigantic king-sized bed.

"Let's see the other rooms," Allison said, dashing for another set of doors.

"This bathroom is as big as a football field," I gasped as I opened the door to the bathroom.

"Randy! Look at this!" Al's voice rang out from the other room. "I think it's a water bed!"

"Get a load of this bathtub!" I called out. "It's as big as a swimming pool!"

We spent the next half hour just running around the suite and trying everything out.

"It's like having our own apartment." Katie laughed as she bounced around on the huge pink bed.

"Except we don't have to cook!" I squealed, throwing a pillow up in the air. "There's no kitchen!"

But just as I said that, I remembered how

hungry I was.

"Oh, no!" I gasped. "Dinner! We forgot all about dinner. We were supposed to meet Miss Munson in the lobby at six-thirty!"

Allison frantically looked at her watch. "It's too late now," she said. "I got so involved, I forgot to set my wrist alarm!"

"And I'm starving!" Randy moaned. "Maybe we can still make it."

"Miss Munson won't be there now. And besides, we'll never have enough time to order and eat," Katie reminded us.

"Hey. What's this?" I asked, walking over to a small cabinet by the dresser.

"It's not a bureau," Katie said, coming over to inspect it. "Look at this. It's all sealed up."

"I'll bet it's a refrigerator," Randy suggested.

"So why is it sealed up?" I questioned.

"It's probably like that banner they have across the toilet seat," Allison informed us. "They probably just clean everything out to get it ready for the next guest."

Curious, I broke the seal and opened the door. "Hey! It *is* a refrigerator! We're saved!" I cheered. "And it's full of food! The seal is probably there to keep everything fresh."

It was filled to the brim with things like cheese, crackers, nuts, sodas, and chocolate bars.

"Who needs dinner?" Randy said, pulling out a bottle of mineral water. "We can have a party right here."

"Right in our very own *suite*," Katie said, a package of crackers in her hand, as she swung her feet up onto the bed.

"This sure beats camping," I said, helping myself to a pack of exotic-looking cheese.

While we raided the refrigerator, we also unpacked and dressed for the play.

This time I made sure I would pass inspection with our teachers. I wore my gray-striped dropped-waist dress and black pumps. Luckily I had brought along my black bolero sweater jacket. I checked myself in the mirror. I put on a little lip gloss, used Katie's nail polish remover to get rid of my yellow-gold nail polish, and was set.

Even Randy got into dressing up. She chose a flared black corduroy skirt with a yellow sweater and a matching black corduroy jacket. Allison and Katie didn't even have to change. They just brushed their hair, unpacked their clothes, and kept snacking.

"Hey, how about some music?" Randy said

as she turned on the radio in the corner of the sitting room.

Believe it or not, the first song we heard was Dylan's new hit, "You're the One."

It reminded me that we still didn't have a plan to meet him. I was just trying to figure out what to do about it when Katie gasped and sounded like she was choking on a cracker.

"Here, drink this," Randy said, quickly handing her a bottle of mineral water.

By then we had all rushed over to where she stood, right next to the refrigerator. She wasn't choking anymore, but she still looked sort of pale.

"Are you all right?" I said. "Do you want us to call a teacher?"

"I'm fine," Katie said after another long sip of water, "but take a look at this. . . ."

She handed Randy this little folder. I had noticed it before on top of the refrigerator, but I didn't bother to look inside. I peered over Randy's shoulder. There was a list of everything inside the refrigerator, and next to the item, a price.

As I read down the list of prices, I felt like I was going to choke, too. "Two dollars for a Milky

Way bar! Two dollars for a can of diet soda! Three-fifty for a little pack of peanuts!" I read out loud.

"And it says here that when we check out, the price of everything we ate will be added to our bill," Randy added.

"Hey! Everybody! Stop chewing!" I blurted out. My friends just looked at me like I was crazy.

"Too late now," Allison said with a shrug. "I guess even candy bars are expensive in a fancy hotel like this one."

I just looked at her while the last peanut stuck in my throat. Unfortunately, she was right.

Chapter Nine

"Sabs, wake up," I heard Katie whisper as I slowly opened my eyes. For a moment I couldn't remember where I was. Then I looked around the hotel room and groaned.

"Oh, no, Katie," I pleaded, "not yet." I pulled the huge feather pillow over my head.

"Sabs, I think there's someone at the door," she whispered, trying to shake me awake.

. "Well, tell them to go away," I moaned, rubbing my eyes. "Aren't we in enough trouble already? I think it would be safer if we just stayed in bed for the rest of the weekend," I sighed as I rolled to the other side of the giant pink bed.

And I really meant it, too. As if the whole thing about the refrigerator hadn't been bad enough, our evening at the theater had been a total mess, too. I mean, it was really exciting going to a famous theater like the Guthrie, and all. But the play had been really boring.

First of all, the actors all had thick British accents, and I couldn't understand them well enough to figure out what was going on. They sounded like they had marbles in their mouths. I had to keep asking Allison what they were saying.

I ended up whispering to Allison for the whole first act! Then everyone around us started hushing me.

During the second act the lady behind us complained to the usher. I almost died when she stuck her stupid flashlight in my face and told me that I had to stand in the lobby for the rest of the play.

Not that I was the only one out there. Nick Robbins had gotten in trouble for snoring, and of course Sam got into trouble, too. There was this one actor who kept lowering his voice throughout the whole thing. Sam got annoyed and yelled out, "Turn up the volume!" like he always does at the movies.

So, during intermission, Miss Miller personally dragged Sam out of his seat by his shirt collar. She really seemed to have it in for him.

But I couldn't believe my eyes when I saw

Allison coming out to the lobby. Her wrist alarm had started beeping and she couldn't turn it off, so Ms. Nelson had told her she had to leave the theater. I felt really bad for poor Al because I knew she had been enjoying the play.

By the time the last act was over, half the class were standing in the lobby, with Mr. Grey watching over us. It was one of the longest nights I had ever spent.

It was only Saturday morning, and so far this whole trip had been one disaster after another. What could happpen next?

"Who's at the door at this hour?" Randy asked, padding into the room. She was wearing zebra-striped pajamas and a giant pair of fuzzy leopard slippers.

"I'll get it," I said, slipping into my white terry-cloth robe as I walked to the door. "It's probably Miss Munson giving me five points off for poor sleeping deportment.

"Who is it?" I asked without opening the door.

"I have a delivery from Musically Yours Music Shop," said the voice on the other side.

"Hmm," Randy pondered, coming up behind me.

"It's for Mr. Dylan Palmer," the voice continued.

My heart skipped a beat. Wide-eyed, I turned around and looked at Randy.

"Open the door!" Katie squealed, tiptoeing up behind her.

"What's going on?" Allison sleepily asked, trailing behind Katie.

I took a deep breath and opened the door to find a bellhop holding up a black guitar case with a bunch of tags hanging from it. Placing the guitar against the wall, he fumbled in his pocket for a pencil.

"This is Mr. Palmer's suite, isn't it?" he asked, staring at Randy's slippers with a puzzled look on his face.

Randy gave me a little kick in the ankle to make me start talking.

"Uh . . . oh, yes. YES!" I piped up. "This is Mr. Suite's Palmer . . . Dylan. We're his . . . daughters," I squeaked.

"His nieces," Randy said at the same time.

"We're Mr. Palmer's nieces . . . daughters," Randy corrected quickly. She grabbed the pencil out of the bellhop's hand. "Where do I sign?"

"R-r-right here," he hesitantly muttered as he

slowly picked up the guitar and indicated a big yellow tag. "The man from the shop has been up all night working on this guitar. He said Mr. Palmer absolutely had to have his guitar in time for rehearsal early this morning," he informed us as Randy signed the tag. "Will you ladies please make sure he gets it as soon as possible?"

"OH, YES!" we all shouted in unison.

Startled, he took a step back from the door. "Are you sure this is Mr. Palmer's suite?" he repeated, looking at the door number.

"Yes, sir. Job well done. Have a nice day!" Randy said quickly. She handed him the tag, pulled the guitar into the room, and closed the door in his face.

"Let me touch it!" I screeched, grabbing the guitar from Randy's grip.

"Be careful," she scolded me. "Let's get it inside and put it on the bed."

"Do you believe this?" I squealed as I carefully laid it down. I unbuckled the guitar case. Inside was Dylan Palmer's trademark ruby-red guitar.

"We must be dreaming," Katie whispered.

"That really is his guitar," Allison confirmed, staring at it in amazement. "I recognize it from the pictures."

"Well, what do we do with it?" Katie questioned.

"We return it to him . . . in person!" I sighed, clasping my hands together and falling on the bed beside it. "It's the perfect way to meet him!"

"But what room is he in, Einstein?" Randy shot back.

"Oh, yeah," I muttered. "What room is he in?"

"Well, he can't be too far," Allison said. "Obviously there's been some kind of room mix-up. But I'll bet he's on this floor."

"Eeeee!" Katie and I screamed at the same time.

"Now all we've got to do is figure out where," Randy said in a very serious tone.

"He needs his guitar as soon as possible. And we're supposed to meet everyone in the restaurant for breakfast in an hour," Katie nervously reminded us.

"Then we've got a lot of work to do in a very short time," I said, springing to my feet. "Let's get dressed first!"

Racing around the suite in a frenzy, we all took showers and changed. I was really glad I had laid out my clothes the night before.

I wore my navy blue sailor dress with white tights and my new red shoes.

Randy wore her black angora sweater with a white miniskirt and black tights, with simple black flats. It was pretty obvious she didn't want to get any more points taken off for "not meeting trip standards."

"Now, where do we start?" Katie asked, coming out of the bathroom with her blow dryer.

She was wearing her pink-and-cream three-piece sweater outfit. Like I said, Dylan just doesn't like pastels. But Katie looked so great, I decided not to say anything.

"Maybe we should call the desk," Al suggested. She was dressed in a purple-and-black suit. She had decided to wear her hair loose, instead of in her usual braid. It looked thick and shiny.

"The desk won't tell us anything," Randy said as she applied a glob of sculpting gel to her spiky black bangs. "And besides that, we never should have signed for the guitar in the first place."

"Randy's right," Al agreed. "There's no point in making any more trouble for ourselves."

"The only thing I can think of is just to go

around and knock on doors," Katie offered.

"But there must be twenty rooms on this floor," Al said. "Knocking on doors would take all day."

"There has to be some way we can find him," I said, wishing for a brainstorm.

I had to figure something out. I just had to. How could I come so close to Dylan — have his very own guitar in my hands — and not get to meet him? All I really needed was one tiny but truly great idea. Was that so much to ask?

Suddenly we heard a big crash. It seemed like the people in the suite next to us had started arguing, and they were getting louder by the minute. Finally the noise got so loud, I just had to find out what was going on.

"I wonder what's going on?" I asked Katie. "Let's go and see what's happening."

Before anyone tried to stop me, I ran to the door. I stepped out into the hallway and started to inch my way toward the suite next door. Out of the corner of my eye I saw something moving and turned to see Katie, Randy, and Al right behind me. Now we moved even slower as a group down the hall. It seemed like ages, but soon we were standing in front of the suite next door with our ears pressed against the door.

"I think I hear someone coming," I whispered. I could hear the footsteps getting closer.

"WELL, WHERE IS THE BLOOMIN' THING?" I heard a voice yell in a thick English accent.

"They're English!" Katie squealed, and grabbed my hand. "You don't think . . ." she began.

"THEY SAID IT WOULD BE HERE ON TIME!" the voice on the other side boomed, just as the door flew open.

Startled, we jumped back. Suddenly we were face to face with the biggest, hairiest man I had ever seen. He looked like Bigfoot.

He must have been nearly seven feet tall, and just as wide. He had long brown hair, a scraggly beard, a gold earring in his nose, and he was wearing a red T-shirt that said DYLAN ON TOUR in big gold letters.

"'Ello!" he snarled.

I felt like I was going to faint. The four of us just stood there and stared at him in shock. He just had to be one of Dylan's bodyguards.

He seemed a little startled by us, too.

"Can I 'elp you ladies?" he asked in a quieter tone.

"This . . . is Mr. Palmer's suite . . . isn't it?" I stammered.

He nodded.

"Well, uh . . . we have his guitar," I said quickly.

Bigfoot's eyes widened. I wasn't sure if he wanted to hit us or kiss us.

"We just got it a few minutes ago!" Randy piped up. "Actually it must have been seconds ago? Right?" she asked. Al, Katie, and I nodded our heads up and down.

"They delivered it to our room by mistake," Allison added.

Bigfoot let out a sigh of relief.

"Thank goodness. I was afraid the boss was gonna 'ave our heads for that one." He sighed again. He pulled out a huge red handkerchief and began mopping his brow. "Well, if you have the guitar, can I see it?"

We turned and made a mad dash for our room. I flung open the door and grabbed the guitar. I was so excited, I almost dropped it. Then we ran right back. Bigfoot was nowhere in sight. But the door was open.

"Do you think we ought to go in?" Katie questioned.

"Probably not," Randy decided. "We don't want to blow it."

So we just stood outside and peeked in. There were a bunch of people inside, but I couldn't be sure that Dylan was one of them. There were clothes and shoes and pieces of musical equipment all over the place. I kept trying to catch a glimpse of Dylan, but I never did.

Just then Bigfoot returned.

"Here's Dylan's guitar," I said, doing my best to sound casual as I handed over the black case.

"Thanks, girls. Dylan will be happy to see this." He took the guitar case slowly out of my hands. Then he looked down at us and smiled.

"My, my, you little lasses certainly are cute," he said. "I imagine you're 'ere for the concert tonight?"

Suddenly I didn't know what to say.

"No. We got in too late to get tickets," Katie cut in.

"Well, we'll 'ave to remedy that right away," Bigfoot responded, drawing himself up to his full height. "I'll go see if I can find some tickets."

"But I thought the entire stadium was sold out, " I blurted out.

"Not all the tickets go on sale, " Bigfoot said

with another aren't-you-cute smile. "Dylan always gets tickets to give out to his friends." And he disappeared back into the suite.

"*Friends*," I echoed in a dreamlike trance. I always knew I was Dylan's number one fan, but now, to be considered one of his actual *friends* . . . I knew for sure that I was dreaming.

A moment later Bigfoot returned and handed me an envelope full of tickets.

"'Ere you are, ten tickets, front row, center. Think that will be enough?"

Mentally I started counting Sam and his friends. And Winslow. And Arizonna! Stacy would be green!

"Front row, center," I heard Katie quietly gasp behind me.

"Ten is just . . . just *perfect*, thank you," I stammered. "Thank you so much."

"Have fun tonight," Bigfoot said cheerfully. Then he stepped back into the suite and shut the door behind him.

I was so overwhelmed, I just kept staring down at the tickets, and then looking back at the door.

We stood there staring at Dylan's hotel door for another five minutes. Then, almost like we were all the same person, we took a deep breath at exactly the same time.

We were in such shock, no one could say anything as we walked down the hall.

"Somebody pinch me," I said when we closed the door to our suite. "I *know* I'm still dreaming."

Chapter Ten

"This is absolutely the most awesome thing that has ever happened to me in my entire life!" I said, collapsing into the nearest chair.

"Let me see those," Randy said, taking the envelope from my hand.

"Stacy Hansen, eat your heart out!" she shouted, and kissed the tickets one by one.

Just at that moment Al's wrist alarm went off again.

"Oh, no!" Al moaned.

"What's wrong?" Katie asked.

"I forgot to fix this thing," she said, smacking the watch face with her hand.

"Don't tell me . . ." I sighed, looking at the clock and quickly coming back down to earth. "You don't mean . . ."

"Sorry," Al said, giving us all an apologetic look. "We missed breakfast . . . and if we don't get out of here in about two minutes, we're going to miss the tour bus!"

"Let's keep the tickets a secret until we get permission to go," I told the girls as we rode down in the elevator.

We were going to get free time to do whatever we wanted after dinner, but our activities had to be approved by a teacher.

Moments later we were boarding the bus. I was looking forward to sightseeing and to visiting the museums on today's agenda. But I just couldn't get my mind off the concert. Tonight I was going to see the man of my dreams, Dylan Palmer!

The morning at the museum flew by. When we stopped at the Sculpture Garden for a picnic at about eleven-thirty, I was starving.

"Don't forget to pick up my box lunch," I begged Katie as I handed her my meal voucher. "I'm going to go talk to Mr. Grey."

Mr. Grey was in charge of giving out passes to the Science Museum, so I had to wait a long time before I got to talk to him.

"I'm very impressed, Miss Wells," he said after I told him what happened. "But you do realize that you're going to need a chaperone."

My face fell. We had just enough tickets to

invite our friends. But now I would have to give one to a chaperone instead.

"But don't worry," Mr. Grey said, smiling down at me. "It's already been decided that I'll be using Stacy's fifth ticket. So I'll just be your chaperone as well. You can ask whomever you'd like."

Now I was angry. Stacy must have known all along that she *really* didn't have an extra ticket. She was just playing it up to drive us all crazy! Now I was totally determined to keep everything a secret until the very last minute. I asked Mr. Grey if he could keep quiet about these extra tickets, even to Stacy. I told him that I didn't want the word to get out and then have the other kids feeling bad that they couldn't go, too. Mr. Grey agreed and I went to join my friends.

Before we got back on the bus, I told the girls that we had gotten the go-ahead. Now we could invite the other kids. I couldn't wait to tell Sam! And I couldn't wait to tear into that delicious box lunch. We were having fried chicken and coleslaw and chocolate cake. Even though I'm always watching my calories, I decided that under the circumstances I would eat every last bite.

"Okay, where's my lunch?" I asked Katie as I sat on the bench beside her.

"Sorry, Sabs," she said, pulling out my meal voucher. "But Miss Munson wouldn't allow me to pick it up. She said only one box lunch per person."

"Oh, no!" I wailed, taking the voucher from Katie's hand. "I'm starving!"

I ran to Miss Munson and handed her my meal voucher. She let me have my lunch, and almost took another five points off my grade for not being "prompt," until I explained that I had been talking with Mr. Grey.

Luckily we were so busy, the afternoon went fast. We went to the Science Museum, and we also got to go to the Minneapolis Zoological Garden.

By the time I knew it, we were back in our suite, dressing for dinner and after that . . . the concert!

I wore my navy blue mini with a blue-green silk T-shirt, and my gold bolero sweater jacket. Randy lent me two of her gold necklaces, and I borrowed a pair of gold knot earrings from Katie. I really looked elegant.

Both Katie and Al wore linen suits. Katie's

was red, and Allison's was kind of a mustardy gold. It looked great with her long black hair.

Of course, Randy wore black. But her miniskirt had a white Op Art pattern running along the hem of the skirt. With her black silk turtleneck shirt and a matching jacket with the same Op Art border on its sleeves, she looked like she really belonged in the big city.

Tonight, of course, we didn't raid the refrigerator — not even a tiny bottle of mineral water. We figured out how much we would owe on our bill and decided we could pay it using money we had brought along for souvenirs. We weren't thrilled about the solution, but we were so excited about the concert, it didn't seem to matter.

Feeling great, we piled into the elevator and headed downstairs for dinner. In the lobby we met Sam and his friend Nick.

"Sure you have our tickets, Sabs?" Sam asked me.

"Don't worry. They're safe and sound," I assured him, patting my purse.

Tonight we were having dinner in the hotel's main dining room, the Monaco Grill. It was really elegant, with crystal glasses, china, and flowers on the tables. All around the room there were huge oil paintings in gold frames. It almost looked like a museum.

The moment we walked in, we were greeted by the maître d'. We learned in one of our classes that the maître d' is the headwaiter in a fancy restaurant. He was a slim, silver-haired man in a black tuxedo. His thin little mustache looked like it was drawn on with an eyeliner pencil.

"We're with the Bradley school," Allison said.

"Of course, right this way," he said. He started to lead us across the room, then noticed that Sam wasn't wearing a jacket.

"I'm sorry, sir," he said very solemnly. "But gentlemen are requested to wear a tie and jacket."

Sam just made a face and shrugged. He was dressed for the concert, wearing a blue pin-striped shirt, a white tie, and black chinos.

"If you wish, sir," the maître d' continued, "we could provide a jacket for you."

"Good idea," Sam said. Then they both disappeared into the coatroom. Another waiter came over and showed us to our table.

There were several tables reserved for our class. Each teacher was sitting at a different table, and we had Miss Miller.

Tonight's dinner was a huge buffet, set out on long tables across one wall of the restaurant. We were allowed to get up and help ourselves to different courses. All the food was arranged in these really neat displays. It almost looked too pretty to eat. But of course we did.

"Wow! This looks great," Katie said as we returned to our table with our plates. "I'm going to try a taste of everything."

"I'm starved, too," Allison said.

I was just about to dig into a delicious-looking slice of beef Wellington — which was like roast beef with some piecrust around it — when Sam showed up. He pulled out his chair and angrily sat down with a thump.

The maître d' had found him a jacket, all right. But it was about ten sizes too big and bright yellow houndstooth check. The sleeves were so long, they flopped around like crazy, and there didn't seem to be much Sam could do to control them.

Everyone in our class cracked up, including Mr. Grey. The whole restaurant was staring at us. Miss Miller looked mortified. Her face got as red as her plaid dress.

"Mr. Wells, you may help yourself to the buffet now," she said. The tone of her voice made us all settle down.

When Sam got up and walked across the room, it was hard not to crack up all over again. But we forced ourselves to look down at our plates and ignore him.

The food really did look great, but I was so excited I could hardly eat a bite. At the next table Stacy and her friends kept looking over at us, whispering, then cracking up. But not out loud, because that would be bad manners and they'd get points deducted.

"Stacy and her friends are such creeps. I think they're laughing at us," Katie observed as she dug her spoon into a dish of chocolate mousse.

"But we'll have the last laugh tonight," Randy said with a gleeful grin. "That's for sure."

Finally dinner was over, and we were waiting at the front of the hotel for our bus to arrive. Some kids were going to the movies with Ms. Nelson, and another bunch were going to the Nicollet Mall with Miss Munson. Miss Miller had decided to stay at the hotel.

Stacy, Eva, B.Z., and Laurel sauntered onto the bus, still laughing at their private joke.

All of the kids we'd invited to the concert sat on the bus looking sad and forlorn. But we had planned it that way.

Stacy kept bragging about her tickets the whole way. She was in her glory.

"Are you guys going to the mall?" she asked as we approached the stop.

We just shook our heads no.

She went back to chatting with Laurel about the concert.

"What movie are you going to see?" she asked sarcastically a little while later.

"We're not going to the movies," Katie replied calmly.

Stacy looked puzzled.

"They're probably going bowling or something," I heard B.Z. say to Eva.

At last the bus ambled on to the Metrodome. It was pretty obvious that Stacy and her clones couldn't figure out why there was still a busload of people. There were the four of us, Sam, Nick, Billy, Arizonna, Winslow, and Jason.

"Here we are, the Metrodome," Mr. Grey called out like a train conductor. "Even I'm excited about this part of the trip."

"Finally," Stacy sighed dramatically. "I

thought we'd never get here."

"Okay, gang, last stop. Everybody out," Mr. Grey instructed us.

"*Everybody?* What are you talking about?" Stacy blurted out. "They don't have tickets!"

"Oh, yes, we do," I calmly replied, pulling the tickets from my purse. "Front row, center," I added with a smile.

Stacy's jaw dropped. "That's impossible," she shouted. "You're lying! The concert was completely sold out months ago."

"Of regular tickets," Randy corrected her. "But Dylan gets loads of tickets to give out to his *special* fans."

"Like us," Allison added.

"Ever since we returned his guitar to his suite this morning," Katie finished.

"I don't believe a word of this," Stacy said with her arms folded over her chest and her eyes narrowed.

"See for yourself," I said, fanning the tickets out in front of her nose, just close enough for her to read them.

She stared down at them for a second. Then her face got redder than the giant cherry at the Sculpture Garden. She looked like she was just about to explode. It was truly a great moment.

"Those seats are even better than mine!" she gasped.

"What did you think?" Randy said with a cool shrug. "Dylan's not going to stick his friends up in the balcony."

"Well, I —" Stacy looked totally flustered. "Oh, never mind!" she said finally and just turned on her heel and stomped away, with her little band of followers behind her.

Stacy and her friends were nowhere to be seen. Obviously their seats were not as great as she had claimed.

Then, without warning, the lights went down and the stadium was pitch-black.

An announcer's voice said, "Ladies and gentlemen, the Metrodome is proud to present . . . that *outrageous* rocker . . . Dylan Palmer!"

We jumped up out of our seats and the screams from the crowd were absolutely deafening. Clouds of white smoke started rising from the dark stage, with blue and purple lights floating in the background.

Then, out of the swirls of smoke, Dylan appeared like a magician or something. He was dressed all in white with knee-high silver boots and silvery fringe on his shirt and pants.

He ran across the stage, waving his ruby-red guitar above his head. A bright spotlight followed him until he was right in front of us. I thought I was going to faint right on the spot. But I held myself together because I didn't want to miss one microsecond of the show.

He strummed his guitar and took a step closer to the microphone. The other members of his band were all standing in their places.

"This is a new song of ours called 'You're the One,'" Dylan said in his dreamy voice. "I'd like to dedicate it to those great girls in suite twenty-three, who did a real good deed this morning. I hope you're out there enjoying the show —"

My friends and I were jumping up and down and screaming at the top of our lungs. Dylan Palmer had actually dedicated a song to us! And then he was singing it in that gorgeous voice of his: ". . . You're the only one for me. Strange destiny . . . "

He looked out into the audience and right at me. Our gazes met and Dylan's wonderful green eyes were looking right into mine as he sang.

". . . When I look into your eyes, I'm hypnotized. *Mesmerized . . ."*

I knew there were thousands of people in the audience, but for a moment I really felt like Dylan was singing only to me.

The rest of the concert was incredible. I'll never forget it as long as I live. It was the best thing that had ever happened to me. It was better than showing up Stacy and her friends. It was even better than getting the free tickets in the first place.

It was absolutely the most *awesome* thing that had *ever* happened in my entire life.

Don't miss
GIRL TALK #21
BABY TALK

"Allison! Where were you this morning? Why weren't you in homeroom?" Sabrina burst out. Her hazel eyes looked like they were about to pop out of her head. She was wearing a hot pink turtleneck that matched the two bright spots on her cheeks exactly.

"Is everything okay?" asked Katie, tucking her blond hair behind her ears and looking concerned.

I sighed. "Things were really busy at home," I explained. "I just couldn't seem to get out of the house on time."

"Now you sound like me!" said Sabrina, laughing. Sabs is always saying that she's late due to reasons beyond her control, and I have to admit, I was beginning to understand what she meant.

Just then Randy walked over with her lunch tray and put it down next to Sabrina.

"Hey, look who it is!" she exclaimed, putting one hand up to her forehead and pretending to be shocked to see me. "Allison Cloud — returned from the land of the lost!"

"Hi, Randy," I said, smiling.

Randy grinned. "I think we'd definitely better call the newspapers about this one. I can see the headlines now: ALLISON CLOUD, LATE FOR SCHOOL."

Sabrina giggled.

"I know, I know," I said, smiling, "but I couldn't help it. My mother was resting, and I was supposed to get Charlie ready for school. But first he knocked over a plant, and I couldn't seem to keep him quiet, and then we couldn't find his sneakers, and then it turned out he forgot his lunch and I had to ride over to the elementary school and drop it off."

. "Wow," said Randy, "sounds like you had your hands full."

"I know what that's like," said Katie, taking a bite of her apple. "When my mother was planning her wedding to Jean-Paul, things were really busy at my house. For a while it seemed like my family only noticed I was there when they needed me to run an errand or something. And then after my mother and Jean-Paul got back from their honeymoon, we had to pack up everything in our old house and move. I was so busy just trying to keep up with it all that half the time I didn't have time to think."

I smiled at Katie. I knew it hadn't been easy for her when her mother remarried. Suddenly she had not only a new stepfather, but a new stepbrother and a new home, too. It seemed like she understood just how I was feeling.

"Hey," said Sabs, "speaking of moving, have you come up with any ideas for your new room yet, Allison?"

LOOK FOR THE AWESOME GIRL TALK BOOKS
IN A STORE NEAR YOU!

Fiction
  #1 WELCOME TO JUNIOR HIGH!
  #2 FACE-OFF!
  #3 THE NEW YOU
  #4 REBEL, REBEL
  #5 IT'S ALL IN THE STARS
  #6 THE GHOST OF EAGLE MOUNTAIN
  #7 ODD COUPLE
  #8 STEALING THE SHOW
  #9 PEER PRESSURE
 #10 FALLING IN LIKE
 #11 MIXED FEELINGS
 #12 DRUMMER GIRL
 #13 THE WINNING TEAM
 #14 EARTH ALERT!
 #15 ON THE AIR
 #16 HERE COMES THE BRIDE
 #17 STAR QUALITY
 #18 KEEPING THE BEAT
 #19 FAMILY AFFAIR
 #20 ROCKIN' CLASS TRIP

Nonfiction
ASK ALLIE: 101 answers to your questions about boys, friends, family, and school!
YOUR PERSONALITY QUIZ: Fun, easy quizzes to help you discover the real you!

TALK BACK!

TELL US WHAT YOU THINK ABOUT GIRL TALK

Name _____

Address _____

City _____ State _____ Zip _____

Birthday Day _____ Mo. _____ Year _____

Telephone Number (___) _____

1) On a scale of 1 (The Pits) to 5 (The Max), how would you rate Girl Talk?   Circle One:

       1   2   3   4   5

2) What do you like most about Girl Talk?

___Characters___Situations___Telephone Talk

Other _____

3) Who is your favorite character? Circle One:

    Sabrina   Katie   Randy

    Allison   Stacy   Other

4) Who is your least favorite character?

_____

5) What do you want to read about in Girl Talk?

_____

_____

Send completed form to :
Western Publishing Company, Inc.
1220 Mound Avenue Mail Station #85
Racine, Wisconsin 53404